"You aren't going to marry Jillian!"

"Is that so?" Zach muttered dangerously.

Jillian tried to plead with her sister to keep quiet, but she wouldn't be stopped. "Jillian told Mother and me that you wouldn't have her even after she threw herself at you!"

Humiliated beyond endurance, Jillian groaned. "Camille, please—"

"You think I didn't sleep with her because I didn't want to?" Zach asked incredulously. "Let me tell you, I didn't sleep with Jillian because I respect her too much. And you have nothing to say about me marrying her. Does she, Jillian?"

"You don't have to go through with it," Jillian replied instead, praying that he'd declare with heartfelt sincerity that he wanted nothing more than to spend the rest of his life with her.

Instead, Zach took a deep breath, his eyes full of apology and regret. "You know I wouldn't insist if it wasn't the only solution. For now."

For now. Jillian blinked back tears and nodded. Only for now.

Dear Reader,

The wonder of a Silhouette Romance is that it can touch *every* woman's heart. Check out this month's offerings—and prepare to be swept away!

A woman wild about kids winds up tutoring a single dad in the art of parenthood in *Babies, Rattles and Cribs... Oh, My!* It's this month's BUNDLES OF JOY title from Leanna Wilson. When a Cinderella-esque waitress—complete with wicked stepfamily!— finds herself in danger, she hires a bodyguard whose idea of protection means making her his *Glass Slipper Bride,* another unforgettable tale from Arlene James. Pair one highly independent woman and one overly protective lawman and what do you have? The prelude to *The Marriage Beat,* Doreen Roberts's sparkling new Romance with a HE'S MY HERO cop.

WRANGLERS & LACE is a theme-based promotion highlighting classic Western stories. July's offering, Cathleen Galitz's *Wyoming Born & Bred,* features an ex-rodeo champion bent on reclaiming his family's homestead who instead discovers that home is with the stubborn new owner...and her three charming children! A long-lost twin, a runaway bride...and *A Gift for the Groom*—don't miss this conclusion to Sally Carleen's delightful duo ON THE WAY TO A WEDDING.... And a man-shy single mom takes a chance and follows *The Way to a Cowboy's Heart* in this emotional heart-tugger from rising star Teresa Southwick.

Enjoy this month's selections, and make sure to drop me a line about *why* you keep coming back to Romance. We want to fulfill *your* dreams!

Happy reading,

Mary-Theresa Hussey

Mary-Theresa Hussey
Senior Editor, Silhouette Romance
300 East 42nd Street, 6th Floor
New York, NY 10017

Please address questions and book requests to:
Silhouette Reader Service
U.S.: 3010 Walden Ave., P.O. Box 1325, Buffalo, NY 14269
Canadian: P.O. Box 609, Fort Erie, Ont. L2A 5X3

VIRGIN BRIDES

GLASS SLIPPER BRIDE

Arlene James

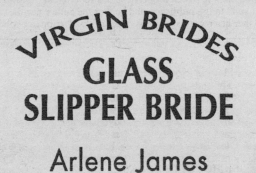

 Silhouette
R O M A N C E ™

Published by Silhouette Books

America's Publisher of Contemporary Romance

SILHOUETTE BOOKS

ISBN 0-373-19379-3

GLASS SLIPPER BRIDE

Books by Arlene James

Silhouette Romance

City Girl #141
No Easy Conquest #235
Two of a Kind #253
A Meeting of Hearts #327
An Obvious Virtue #384
Now or Never #404
Reason Enough #421
The Right Moves #446
Strange Bedfellows #471
The Private Garden #495
The Boy Next Door #518
Under a Desert Sky #559
A Delicate Balance #578
The Discerning Heart #614
Dream of a Lifetime #661
Finally Home #687
A Perfect Gentleman #705
Family Man #728
A Man of His Word #770
Tough Guy #806
Gold Digger #830
Palace City Prince #866
*The Perfect Wedding #962
*An Old-Fashioned Love #968
*A Wife Worth Waiting For #974
Mail-Order Brood #1024
*The Rogue Who Came To Stay #1061
*Most Wanted Dad #1144
Desperately Seeking Daddy #1186
*Falling for a Father of Four #1295
A Bride To Honor #1330
Mr. Right Next Door #1352
Glass Slipper Bride #1379

Silhouette Special Edition

A Rumor of Love #664
Husband in the Making #776
With Baby in Mind #869
Child of Her Heart #964
*The Knight, the Waitress
   and the Toddler* #1131
Every Cowgirl's Dream #1195
Marrying an Older Man #1235

Silhouette Books

Fortune's Children
Single with Children

*This Side of Heaven

ARLENE JAMES

grew up in Oklahoma and has lived all over the South. In 1976 she married "the most romantic man in the world." The author enjoys traveling with her husband, but writing has always been her chief pastime.

Dear Reader,

Don't you just love to discover some hidden strength or goodness in yourself? It makes one feel a certain careful pride and a sense of accomplishment. Unfortunately those discoveries don't come on soft summer days spent in a hammock with a good book and a tall glass of lemonade. Such self-discovery is always the result of some difficulty in our lives, something we feel helpless to face or change. Such is the case with Jillian Waltham.

Like most well-rounded adults, Jillian knows herself better than she realizes. She knows that she has talent and that she's capable of loving selflessly. She even knows what she wants. What she doesn't realize is that she can make others know those things about her, too, even Zachary Keller, the handsome hero who makes all the girls' hearts go pitter-patter.

It's difficulty and the very real threat of danger that brings a hero into Jillian's life to begin with, but it's Jillian herself who provokes him to his very greatest acts of heroism. In doing so, Jillian discovers the depth and value of her true self—and she begins to understand, along with everyone else, that she actually deserves true love as much as, say, Zach Keller.

I hope you enjoy Jillian's journey to her true self and her true love as much as I have.

God bless,

Arlene James

Chapter One

Two broad slices of potato bread, lightly toasted and slathered with honey mustard. Mesquite smoked turkey breast, sliced paper thin, and a slab of lean roast beef. Shredded iceberg and butter lettuce. Tomato, lightly salted. No cheese. A relish of white onion, kosher dill and pickled jalapeño pepper. And for the finishing touch, black olives cut into tiny rings and sprinkled liberally over the whole with just a dash of red wine vinegar.

Jillian pressed the second slice of potato bread carefully over the monstrous sandwich, neatly ''diapered'' it with waxed paper and a toothpick, wrapped it a second time and slipped it into the brown paper sack printed with the words *Downtown Deli*. To the sandwich in the sack she added a small bag of barbecue potato chips, a shiny red delicious apple and a single piece of dark-mint chocolate, which he would eat first instead of last. The lunch safely packed, she poured a large container of strong black coffee, capped it with a lid and placed both lunch sack and coffee container in a cardboard punch-out tray. Now it was time to look to herself.

She washed her hands at the far sink, removed her smudged white apron, smoothed the straight skirt of her pale-gray uniform, pushed her glasses farther up on her nose and patted the head-band with the white paper decoration that declared her a *Downtown Deli Delight* and held back her wispy, caramel-colored hair. She sighed, knowing exactly what she looked like. At five feet ten inches and 130 pounds, she was a gangly, awkward excuse for a woman, with waiflike pale-blue eyes twice the normal size dominating a pointy face more suited to a gnome than a female. Ah, well, Zachary Keller, of Threat Management, Inc., wasn't likely to notice the first thing about her.

She doubted that in the seven weeks since she'd come to work here behind the counter of the deli in his office building he had noticed her even once, despite the fact that she'd built him the same sandwich at least a dozen times. Now she needed his help. She was about to pass from the cipher behind the counter to supplicant and then intermediary. Soon, she suspected, she would be dismissed altogether. The important thing was to engage his interest on Camille's behalf, and she could do that. She could.

So what if her knees went weak every time she saw him? Every tall, hunky, dark-haired, green-eyed, chiseled-faced man did that to her. If she couldn't exactly remember any others, that signified nothing. They hadn't noticed her, either, she was sure. Camille was the one who got noticed, petite, pretty, blond, successful Camille, the Camille who was all the family she had, her much admired, much loved elder sister.

Jillian waved at the counter manager and received his permission to leave in the nod of his balding head. Carrying the cardboard tray, she slid from behind the deli cooler and walked across the tiny dining space toward the bank of elevators across the lobby. Tess, one of her co-workers, paused while wiping down the hubcap-sized glass top of a tiny wrought-iron table recently vacated by two secretaries taking a late coffee break and called out encouragement.

"You go, girl! Get that good-looking man in your corner!"

Jilly laughed and held up crossed fingers. Every female in the building had a crush on the man. His quick smile, enigmatic green eyes and extremely fit, muscular build were the stuff of fantasies, but according to his secretary, Lois—fifty-something, divorced, pragmatic, efficient and talkative—he didn't date much. Some of the girls suspected a deep emotional wound, perhaps even a broken heart.

Jillian stepped into the elevator and punched the seventh-floor button.

At the rap of his secretary's knuckles upon his office door, Zach looked up from the notes from which he was dictating, switched off the recorder and cleared his throat before assuming "the position" by leaning back in his chair and propping one cowboy-booted foot negligently on the corner of his desk. "Yeah?"

The door swung open, and Lois's long, thin face, piled high with too-dark hair, appeared. "Lunch!" she announced brightly.

Zach launched a normally straight eyebrow into an expressive arch as he sat upright and glanced at the black onyx face of his watch. "Bit early, isn't it?"

As often happened, Lois wasn't paying the least attention. Instead, she stood gesticulating at someone out of sight. Resignedly, Zach leaned back once more and lifted both legs to prop them on the corner of his desk, then crossed them at the ankles. Hands folded complacently over his belt buckle, he admired his reddish-brown, round-toed, full-quill ostrich boots and the stiff crease in his dark jeans for a moment, quite sure that whatever was up would soon be forthcoming. Sure enough, a tall, slender woman in a tacky, ill-fitting, gray-and-white uniform and large square glasses appeared in the doorway, holding a cardboard tray. He recognized the bag wedged into one end of the tray, and his mouth watered. The woman took a moment to place—behind the deli counter. She was a lot taller than he'd realized and willow thin, with an interesting, piquant face almost obscured by those huge, hideous glasses. He'd always figured that she was nearsighted, because her eyes could not possibly be that big; they must be distorted by the lenses.

"I didn't order lunch today," he said, pleasant but dismissive. Her small, plump, bow-shaped mouth trembled slightly above her delicately pointed chin. "I know," she admitted breathlessly. "It's a bribe."

He almost laughed, but the seriousness of her expression somehow quelled the impulse. "Policemen can be bribed," he pointed out, "but I'm not a cop any longer, Miss—?" He made it a question.

Lois took over then, saying, "Waltham. It's Jillian Waltham. Jilly, this is my boss, Zachary Keller. Jilly has a problem, Boss, just the sort you manage best. I promised her you'd help."

So that was it, another charity case. For some reason, that irritated him when it never had before. He turned away no one who really needed his help—women, usually, whose mates battered and berated them. Most of his paying clients were celebrities of some sort who needed protection or just "buffering," someone to stand between them and the public. Occasionally, if business was slow, he worked standard security for corporations and organizations, seminars, private banquets and such, but he much preferred helping individual clients remove themselves from danger and dead-end lives. And yet, for some reason, he didn't want to deal with this woman. He didn't want to, but he would.

Zach dropped his feet and leaned forward, reaching for the bag with a smile on his face, as if to say he'd save the world for a Downtown Deli sandwich. "Have a seat, Jillian Waltham, and tell me how I can help you."

She handed over the tray and practically collapsed into the small armchair opposite his desk. "I know I should have made an appointment, but I was afraid it would be weeks before you could see me."

Business was good, but not that good. Thankfully. He waved away the statement with one hand while unfolding the top of the bag with the other. "No problem. We try to be accommodating."

"It's just the way you always order it," she said helpfully, meaning the sandwich.

He shot her a look and moved on to the coffee, lifting the container from the tray and carefully removing the lid before tossing it into the trash basket under his desk. Settling back into his chair once more, he sipped the strong black brew and contemplated the woman opposite him. He was surprised to find that behind those hideous glasses and beneath that laughable headband was an arrestingly pretty face. It was almost elfin. In fact, if her ears were pointed she'd look just like the drawing of a fairy princess in his nephew's book of fairy tales. And, by golly, those enormous eyes were just that. Upon closer inspection, he rather doubted that she really even needed those glasses and their seemingly flat lenses. For some reason that irritated, too. What was she hiding from? *Who* was she hiding from? Or was it something more sinister?

Zach had learned from sad experience that the more controlling, abusive husbands and boyfriends typically belittled the very objects of their desire to the point of self-hatred. It was as if such men could not bear for the world to see what attracted them. Women so beleaguered tended to see themselves as unattractive, frumpy, even ugly, and to present themselves accordingly. He wondered who had convinced Jillian Waltham that she was unattractive.

"Are you married?" he asked, taking a peek at her bare ring finger.

She seemed surprised by the question. "Ah, no."

"Ever been married?"

She frowned. "No."

"It's a boyfriend, then," he surmised authoritatively, "someone who tells you that you don't deserve him and then won't let go. I've seen it dozens of times."

She pushed her glasses up on her short, sharp nose and studied him. Suddenly enlightenment softened her face, and she laughed, a light, chiming sound that seemed to make magic. In that instant she wasn't pretty at all. She was beautiful, breathtakingly so. Zach set his cup down with a muted plunk, hot coffee splashing over the rim onto the webbing between his thumb and forefinger. He shook his hand and rubbed it against his thigh, mesmerized, and suddenly he knew what it was about her that bothered him.

Serena.

Jillian Waltham reminded him of Serena.

He immediately squelched the spurt of emotion that thinking of Serena inevitably brought him. It had been almost five years, and the thought of her senseless death still enraged and pained him. Desperately, he pushed the thought away and tried to listen to Jillian Waltham.

"It isn't *my* boyfriend," she was saying, leaning forward. "It's my sister's."

"Sister's," he echoed dumbly.

"Maybe you've heard of her, Camille Waltham, Channel 3 News."

Camille Waltham. Channel 3 News. Sister. Something familiar swam around the edges of his mind and then suddenly dove into its center. He saw a trim, effervescent, conventionally pretty blonde with smartly styled hair and perfect makeup. The sound of her voice came to him: "This is Camille Waltham, Channel 3 News, thanking you for watching. Because we're YOUR news station." Reality snapped into focus. Not Jillian Waltham. Not someone who reminded him of Serena. And not a charity case, thank God. Camille Waltham, newscaster. He opened a drawer and took out a pad and pen. After flipping open the pad, he began to write.

"Let me get this straight," he said, "someone is threatening your sister."

A brief silence alerted him, and he looked up. Jillian Waltham sat with a pensive expression on her face.

"Not *threatening*, really."

Zach laid down the pen, feeling seriously exasperated.

"It's more like he's *stalking* her."

Ice slid through his veins. Zach picked up the pen, all business now. "Any idea when this started?"

"Oh, yes. When she broke up with him. And it's just like him, too. Janzen never could take no for an answer. It's like putting up a red flag, issuing a challenge. Even if he doesn't want it, he'll go after it just because you told him he couldn't have it."

With a sigh, Zach laid down the pen again and reached for patience. "I really need a date."

"A *date?*"

The squeak in her voice confused him. "Yes, please."

"Well, all right," she said, "but we have to take care of my sister first. She's all the family I have."

He stared at her for several long seconds before all became clear, and then he didn't know whether he was amused or appalled. "Uh, you, um, misunderstand me, I think. What I need is the date your sister broke up with this boyfriend."

"Oh! *That* date!" She laughed, but it was nothing like before, and the red flags of color rose in her cheeks. "I thought...but, I should have known better! You sounded a little desperate there, and a man like you wouldn't..." She laughed again, the sound so strained and false that it made him want to shake her. She must have sensed his mood, for she took a deep breath then and said solemnly, "It was almost two months ago when they broke up. Say, May 8 or 9. Camille would be able to tell you exactly, of course."

Of course. He cleared his throat, uncomfortable with the knowledge that she considered herself beneath him. But that wasn't his problem. He tried to concentrate on business. Question number one. "Why, exactly, am I talking to you about this instead of your sister?"

"Oh, Camille's scheduled for every moment," Jillian said. "You know how it is, the station's always sending her out on public relations stuff. It's that local celebrity thing."

He knew too well the demands made on and by celebrity types. "Okay, then, let's take it from the top, Miss Waltham."

"'Jillian,'" she said.

He nodded.

"Or 'Jilly,' if you prefer."

He didn't prefer, actually. The sobriquet seemed to further trivialize her somehow, but again, it wasn't any of his business. He made himself nod and smile. "Could you start from the beginning, please, and explain exactly why you're here?"

She slid to the very edge of her seat and confided, "It was the broken window."

He opened his mouth to elicit an explanation, then closed it again, hoping that he would do better to let her tell it in her own way. The fallacy of that notion quickly became obvious.

"Camille says it was an accident," Jillian went on, "and it probably was. He's not all that coordinated. I mean, you'd think someone who's involved with music, even if it is just advertising on the radio, could at least dance, you know, but not Janzen— not that he knows it. He doesn't. He thinks he's the world's greatest dancer, just as he thinks he's God's gift to women. So maybe he broke it when he was trying to paint it."

Zach realized he was grinding his teeth and relaxed his jaw to ask, "The window, you mean?"

"Yes."

"He was painting a window?"

"With words," she confirmed.

"Words. Ahha. And what words would those be?"

She shrugged. "I don't know. We couldn't read them after it broke."

"The window, you mean."

"Yes, of course."

Of course. Zach contemplated the container of coffee growing cold on his desk and wondered if it was possible to drown in it. He rejected that particular avenue of escape and sat back again, elbows propped on the arms of his chair, fingers templed. "So your sister broke up with her boyfriend, Janzen, and he tried to write words on her window and probably broke it that way, so no one knows what he was writing."

"Except *you.*"

"*Me?*"

"No, *you.* The word *you.* That part was written on the brick next to the window."

Zach swallowed something hot and acrid that tasted strangely like anger, but he couldn't have said just with whom he was angry at that moment. He rubbed a hand over his face and said, "So he wrote something that ended in the word *you.*"

"Exactly."

Zach waited, but she didn't say anything else; so he thought perhaps he would offer some suggestions. "What do you *think* he wrote? I hate you? I want to kill you?"

She shrugged, not quite meeting his eyes.

"But it was a threat of some kind," he pressed impatiently.

She sighed. "*I* think so."

He floundered helplessly. This obviously was getting them no-where. "I'm afraid I'm going to have to speak with your sister."

Jillian closed her enormous eyes in obvious relief. "Oh, thank you! I'm so worried about her."

He nodded. "Right. So, um, shall I call her?"

"Oh, that won't be necessary," Jillian said. "Just show up around six o'clock."

"Show up?"

"At Camille's."

"You want me to come by her house at six o'clock this eve-ning?"

Delicate, wispy brows drew together. "Is that a problem?"

It wasn't, actually. He often made calls to women's shelters, private offices and police stations, and he could make this one on his way to dinner at his brother's. Why, then, was he looking for excuses not to go? He shook his head. "Just tell me where, exactly, I should show up."

She rattled off an address in North Dallas between the Park Cities and LBJ Freeway. He grabbed the pen and wrote it down in his notebook.

"And your sister—will she be expecting me?"

"Absolutely."

He closed the notebook and laid the pen atop it. "I'll see her, then."

Jillian got up from the chair and attempted to smooth her wrin-kled skirt, saying, "I can't thank you enough, Mr. Keller."

"No problem." He stood and thrust back the sides of his pale, tweed sport jacket to place his hands at his waist. "Thanks for the lunch."

"My pleasure."

He nodded and forced his mouth into a semblance of a smile until she'd maneuvered around the chair and turned toward the door. Then for some reason, without even planning to, he heard himself calling her back. "Jillian."

She turned and blinked owlishly at him. "Yes?"

"About that, um, *date* thing."

Her cheeks immediately flamed pink. "Oh, don't worry about that. It was a silly misunderstanding."

"I know, but it's not that I wouldn't... That is, I have a policy about getting involved with clients. It's not wise. Emotions tend to run high in situations like these, and I can't let myself take advantage of that."

"Of course," she said. "You're a professional."

"Exactly."

She smiled wanly. "I understand."

"Good."

Still smiling, she pushed her glasses up on her nose and went out the door. It had barely closed behind her before he remembered that she wasn't a client at all. Her sister might be, but Jillian Waltham was not. No reason really existed why he couldn't ask her out on a date if he wanted to. Not that he wanted to. He just didn't want her to think that he didn't want to, which didn't really make any sense even to him.

It was the Serena thing, no doubt. Funny that she should put him in mind of Serena, though. She didn't *look* like Serena— well, other than that tall, model's build—and she certainly didn't behave like Serena, who had been quietly confident and well-spoken. No, it was something else. Something he couldn't quite put his finger on just yet.

He sat down and contemplated the brown sack containing the lunch he hadn't ordered, but it was Serena's face he saw. A perfect oval framed by long auburn hair, expressive green eyes, straight, slender nose, a full lush mouth. That face had sold everything from mascara to opera tickets. But as lovely as it had been, it was nothing compared with the loveliness of her soul. Serena had been that rare, true beauty who was as pretty inside as out. And she was gone, killed by a crazed, obsessive fan who had fancied himself somehow rejected by her. As was that naive, cocky young policeman who had fed the threats and complaints into the system, believing that would be enough to protect her. He knew better now.

The system was hamstrung by minutiae and overburdened by the sheer volume of similar cases. The average policeman's hands were literally tied by what seemed to Zach to be nonsensical laws and the unscrupulousness of the criminal population. Law enforcement was an honorable profession, one embraced wholeheartedly by his family, but Serena's loss had convinced him that he could do more by working the system from the outside than the inside, and he had done a lot of good since then. He admitted that without vanity or ego. It was the balm that made old pains bearable.

So why did he recoil from this case? Jillian Waltham wasn't even the target. He probably wouldn't even see her again. Even if he found cause for concern and took the case, he would be protecting Camille Waltham, not her sister—and for pay. Talking news heads tended to make good money, even if they were only local. So it was settled, not that it had been in question, really. He would stop by Camille Waltham's neighborhood and see what she had to say about this broken window and her former boyfriend. If he did take the case, he'd be dealing with Camille. It should be simple enough to stay clear of Jillian's path.

It occurred to him that the whole thing might be blown out of proportion by a nervous sister; Jillian had said that Camille considered the broken window an accident. He'd reserve judgment until he'd heard the whole story. Then, even if Camille did need and want his services, he could see no reason for Jillian to be overly involved.

He felt slightly foolish now. Talk about overreacting! He pictured Jillian Waltham's pixie face behind those big, clunky glasses and laughed at himself. What was he thinking? She was nothing like Serena, really, and she wasn't the target, so he wouldn't have to see her even if he did take the case.

He began to unpack the lunch sack, his stomach growling in anticipation of the treat to come. With Jillian Waltham and her arresting eyes tucked firmly out of mind, he leaned back, propped his feet and dug in.

* * *

When she opened the door and smiled at him, his stomach dropped. The baggy khaki shorts and oversized red camp shirt were not much improvement over that awful deli uniform, and yet she had definitely improved somehow.

"Jillian. I didn't expect to see you here," he said, trying not to study her too closely.

"No? Didn't I tell you that I live here?"

He shook his head. "I thought your sister lived here."

"She does. It's her house. She took me in after my parents died."

Great, he thought. Now how do I keep you out of this? He lifted a hand to the back of his neck. She stepped back and pushed the door open wider.

"Come on in and have a seat."

He could think of no way to refuse and gingerly stepped past her into a cool gold-and-white entry hall with a twelve-foot ceiling and an impressive glass-and-brass light fixture that looked as though it belonged in an ultramodern office building. He followed Jillian down the hall and through a wide doorway on the right. The formal living room was done in shades of white, cream and pale green. It had an unused air about it. She waved him down onto a pristine sofa covered in cream-colored linen and decorated with pale-green fringe before opening a cabinet in one corner, revealing a small bar.

"What can I get you to drink?"

"Nothing, thanks. I'm not much for alcohol."

"Me, neither," she said, opening the door of a tiny refrigerator to reveal rows of canned colas. "But I do like a jolt of cold caffeine on a hot evening."

"In that case, I'll have what you're having."

She removed two cold cans and popped the tops. "Want a glass?"

"Nope."

She carried the colas over to the couch and sat down, offering one to him. He took it carefully, avoiding contact with her fingers.

"Thanks."

"No problem," she said. "You're easy. I don't even have to wash a glass."

"Stays colder in the can," he said, taking a sip.

She nodded and pushed her glasses up on her nose. "Camille's not here right now, but she'll be along in just a minute. The TV station's got her going out to some charity gala tonight, so she had to get a dress."

He filed that away for future reference and turned the conversation to a subject that had been bothering him since she'd mentioned it. "You said that she took you in after your parents died."

Jillian nodded. "That's right. My mom and dad were killed in a boating accident when I was eleven. Camille was only seventeen, but she insisted her mother take me in."

"I thought Camille was your sister."

"She is. My half sister, anyway. We had the same father but different mothers."

"I see."

Jillian nodded and curled one long leg up beneath the other. Her feet were bare, and he couldn't help noticing that they were long and slender with high arches, her second toe longer than the first, the nails oval and neatly trimmed. He wondered irrationally if she would appreciate a good foot rub as much as Serena had after a long photo shoot. To block that train of thought, he searched for something else to say and came up with, "It must seem like you're full sisters if Camille's mother raised you from the age of eleven."

"She didn't," Jillian said, then she seemed surprised that she'd said it. "I mean, Camille was more a second mother to me than Gerry—that is, Geraldine." She grimaced and went on. "Don't misunderstand me. Gerry's been great. It's just that my father left her for my mother, who was his secretary at the time, so naturally she doesn't look on me as another daughter, just her daughter's half sister."

Zach lifted a brow at that. "Must've been awkward, living with your father's ex-wife."

She shrugged. "We've gotten used to it over the years."

"You mean you all still live together?"

"That's right. Only it's Camille's house now. After Gerry's last husband died she moved in with us." Jillian leaned forward then and confessed, "There have been three—husbands, I mean—including my father, who was number one." She sat back. "Anyway, it's a big house."

Her background sure made his look pedestrian. His own parents had been married thirty-six years and currently divided their time between Montana in the summer and Texas in the winter. With one older and one younger brother, both married and settled, both cops like their father, he was the closest thing to a black sheep in the Keller family. Even among all the aunts, uncles and cousins there had been few divorces and fewer deaths. He sipped more cola and thought of another question to keep the conversation going.

"Don't you have any other family?"

Jillian shrugged. "I have an aunt by marriage and a couple of cousins in Wisconsin. My uncle was still living when my father died, but he was disabled, so my aunt really couldn't take on anything else. My mother was an only child born late and unexpectedly in her parents' lives. I don't even remember them. If not for Camille, I'd have been fostered somewhere or sent to an orphanage."

"So she's really all you have," he commented softly.

Jillian nodded. "And I can't let anything happen to her."

Just then a door slammed somewhere in the back of the house. Voices and footsteps could be faintly heard, then a shout. "Jilly!"

Jillian got up and went into the hall. "We're in the living room, Camille."

"We?"

"Zachary Keller and I."

A long silence followed and then someone shouted, "Bring him into the bedroom."

The bedroom? Jillian glanced at Zach and shrugged apologetically. "She's awfully busy, and she does have this public evening out."

He got up. "Maybe I should come back another time."

"Oh, no!" She rushed toward him. "Please at least talk to her."

He wanted to say no, but he couldn't quite look into those huge, worried eyes and manage it. He nodded. "If you're sure she has the time." He took a long drink of the cola and handed it to her. She carried the half-filled can to the bar and left it on the marble countertop.

"Follow me."

She hurried out of the room on her slender, bare feet. He took a deep breath and trailed her across the hall and through a formal dining room, glimpsing a kind of den on the way, and out the other hall into a smallish but well-appointed kitchen, which opened onto yet another hall, where she turned right. She went down the hallway to the end and led him through an open door— into utter chaos.

He got a fleeting impression of lavender and pale green, formal draperies, graceful furnishings and plush white carpet, before the frenetic motion of several bodies moving at once enveloped him. A tall, rawboned woman with ink-black hair scraped into a sophisticated roll on the back of her head swept past him toward the bed, trailing a garment on a hanger. A small man with a gray ponytail trotted by carrying a large white leather case, a rat-tail comb stuck into the clump of hair at his nape. A petite, middle-aged blonde with beauty-shop hair and skin that looked as though it had been stretched too tautly against her skull swayed past in an expensive pink suit, barking orders to the room at large.

"Be careful with those silk stockings," she was saying. "Someone get the beaded handbag and the blue satin shoes. I'll get the sapphires myself."

"Did anyone order flowers?" a man wanted to know. "I was told it was taken care of."

Zach turned his head to find a man in a tuxedo sitting in an armchair beside the bed, calmly thumbing through a magazine.

"I have the flowers," a female said, coming into the room behind Zach, "and the makeup base."

"Thank God!" the man with the ponytail exclaimed, practically bowling over Zach in his hurry to take the small bottle of cosmetics from the blue-jeaned newcomer who brushed past them both. The tuxedo didn't even bother to look up from his magazine.

"Shall I return the rest or keep them on consignment?" the tall woman wanted to know.

"Consignment," said the middle-aged blonde, carrying a pair of shoes in one hand and a sapphire necklace draped over the other.

"I wish we had time to wash this mess," the ponytail complained, yanking free the comb.

"Anyone know when the limo arrives?" asked the tuxedo disinterestedly.

Jillian cupped her hands around her mouth. "Camille?"

The pink blonde turned on her. "Do you have to shout, Jilly? Can't you see your sister's busy?"

Jillian ignored her. "Camille?"

"I'm not a miracle worker, you know," the ponytail said, furiously back-combing someone's hair.

"I could use a cold drink," said the tuxedo.

"I'll get it," said blue jeans, "as soon as I find the evening bag."

"Camille?" Jillian said once more above the general hubbub.

They all ignored her, even the pink blonde, who was busy laying out the sapphire necklace and a pair of matching earrings on the bed. Zachary had had enough. He put two fingers into his mouth and let loose a long, shrill whistle that brought the whole room to an instant stop.

He looked from face to face and failed to find what he was looking for. "I have an appointment with Camille Waltham," he announced in a tone that commanded not only attention but obedience. "Where is she?"

Bodies shifted and drifted, clearing a path through the center of the room. There in front of the massive, multipaned windows stood a small French-provincial dressing table and before it on a tufted stool sat a dainty, fragile woman with the features of a porcelain figurine and vivid blue eyes. Even ratted wildly, her long golden-blond hair made a gleaming halo around her angelic face. She was smaller than he'd imagined and appeared surprisingly vulnerable in a royal-blue silk robe that seemed much too large for her. She looked him over, head to toe, with her calm, vibrant eyes, and then she smiled welcomingly.

His stomach turned over. He glanced almost guiltily at Jillian, who had pushed her glasses up on top of her head, and the very same smile as that aimed at him from across the room curved her mouth.

Double trouble, he thought with ominous confidence—and wondered if it was too late to run.

Chapter Two

Camille Waltham rose regally from the velvet tuft, her dainty feet encased in ridiculously elegant silk slippers with bows on the toes. She smoothed down her wild hair with both hands, then planted her hands at her slender hips and lifted her chin, blue eyes glittering as they held his. Something hovered about her cupid's bow mouth, held at bay by sheer determination. Then she abruptly switched her gaze to his left, targeting Jillian, suddenly imperious.

"You said he was good. You didn't say he was *good-looking*."

The unctuous tone of her voice soured in the pit of Zach's stomach, raising distaste and instant dislike. Good-looking? Was he supposed to be flattered? Even knowing that somehow he would have been, had the comment come from anyone else, didn't make him like the woman any better. Jillian, at least, seemed to realize that her sister's behavior was tasteless. She attempted to normalize the situation by rushing into introductions.

"Zachary Keller, I'd like you to meet my sister, Camille Waltham. Camille, this is Mr. Keller."

Camille at first appeared piqued; then abruptly she floated across the room and offered a small, perfect hand, her gaze measuring him with the efficiency of a laser beam. He wondered if she meant for him to kiss it. Instead, he gave it a brief squeeze and dropped it like a hot potato. Something indecipherable flashed across her face and was quickly replaced by hauteur. She addressed herself to Jillian once again.

"I suppose he would be an acceptable bodyguard." She turned away and floated back toward the dressing table. Casting a coy look over one shoulder, she added, "He'd have to pose as a suitor, of course, a love interest, a boyfriend."

Jillian glanced an apology in his direction and opened her mouth, but he beat her to the reply.

"No way. Out of the question."

Camille Waltham turned back to him almost petulantly. "Oh? And why is that?"

"Because I have a few iron-clad rules concerning my business," he told her, folding his hands and widening his stance, "and number one is that I don't get involved or pretend to be involved—romantically with my clients. Period."

She lifted her chin. "I don't see why—"

"It tends to aggravate the problem, especially in partner abuse cases. Otherwise, it's just bad policy."

She inclined her head. "Surely you can make exceptions for high-profile—"

"No exceptions," he interrupted flatly. "The bottom line is this. If I'm going to help you, you're going to have to do things my way."

"And if I don't?" she challenged mildly.

He shrugged. "I'm the professional here, so I give the orders. If that doesn't work for you, find somebody else to take care of your stalker."

Camille shot a glance at Jillian, then suddenly dropped onto the tuft in front of her dressing table. "Who says I'm being stalked?"

Jillian stepped forward once more, worriedly glancing in Zach's direction. "Camille, you have to take this seriously. You know how Janzen is. He won't just go away, because that's exactly what you want him to do.''

"And whose fault is that?'' the blonde in pink snapped.

Camille turned a resentful glare on the woman, then seemed to subside, leaning an elbow on the edge of the table. "What do you recommend?'' she asked reluctantly.

Zach assumed the question was meant for him.

"For starters,'' he said, "I recommend you send the flunkies out for coffee and give me a few minutes of your undivided attention. Now.''

For a moment he thought, hoped, she would refuse, but then she jerked one hand and the majority of the room's occupants tried to beat one another to the door. Only two remained, Jillian and the blonde in pink. He turned a pointed glare on the blonde, who drew herself up sternly then ruined the effect by sniping pettily at Jillian, "If she can stay, so can I.''

"They both stay,'' said Camille, sounding bored. "Jillian, as you know, is my sister, and this is my mother, Gerry.'' She waved a hand at the pink suit.

"That's 'Geraldine,''' the blonde in pink said, "Geraldine Hunsell Baker.''

"Actually, that's Geraldine Porter Waltham Hunsell Baker,'' Camille said slyly.

Zach made no acknowledgment of the litany of names, not even the two socially prominent ones. Instead, he removed a small notebook and an ink pen from his jacket pocket and prepared to take notes. "All right,'' he said. "Let's have the whole story.''

Camille shrugged and began applying makeup with tiny sponges as she talked, explaining how she had met, dated and eventually become engaged to a once successful but now-unemployed advertising executive named Janzen Eibersen, whom she had allowed to move in with her. According to her, Eibersen had at first seemed to actually enjoy the "public socializing'' that, again according to her, was part of her career. Gradually, however, it became obvious that Janzen had a drinking problem, and he began embarrassing her. They argued, and he drank more.

Absenteeism became a problem on his job, and he was eventually fired. When she broke up with him and threw him out the house, he blamed her with all his problems and vowed that "she wouldn't get away with it."

His "punishment" of her began with repeated phone calls and letters that were returned or destroyed unopened. He had even called her boss to complain that she was trying to control and ruin his life. His latest effort was an act of vandalism that had resulted in a broken window, a sure sign of growing desperation, even though Camille sniggered that it had to have been an accident because Janzen would never risk injuring himself to make a point. She had no idea where to locate Eibersen and had met only a few of his friends. She believed that he would grow tired of the game when he saw that he was not affecting her noticeably and just go away, but for Jillian's sake, she was willing to take the situation more seriously. Jillian, for her part, stood mutely with her arms wrapped around her middle as if holding in something that she desperately wanted to say.

Zach was uncertain what to think, really. Was Janzen dangerous or merely irritating? Had Jillian overreacted, or was Camille downplaying the seriousness of the situation? He knew only one thing for certain: it made no sense to take chances. If Camille was right, she'd have spent some money—which she obviously could afford—for no definite reason. If she was wrong, spending that money on her own security would be the best investment she ever made.

"I'll want to see that window before I go," he said, "but right now I have a few questions."

She waved a hand as if granting him permission to ask what he would while she applied lipstick with a brush.

He tamped down his irritation and focused. "Has this Eibersen ever hit you?"

She considered her reflection in the mirror for a moment, smacked her lips and said, "Not intentionally."

Jillian made a slight movement that he caught with the corner of his eye. Turning his head, he lifted a brow, inviting her to speak. She did so as if explaining for her sister was something she did every day. "Janzen was drunk. He took a swing at Plato, missed and clipped Camille on the chin."

"She could hardly speak for a week," Geraldine said, as though it were somehow Jillian's fault.

"And never missed a newscast," Camille said, batting her eyelashes as she brushed mascara into them.

Zach asked, "Who's Plato?"

"Camille's hairdresser," Jillian answered.

"The gray ponytail? What'd Eibersen have against him?"

Camille capped the mascara and tossed it away. "Jan liked my full attention," she said, giving her full attention to her reflection in the small lit mirror standing atop the dressing table.

Zach could just see a drunken Janzen trying to talk lucidly with a preoccupied Camille while the hairdresser fluttered around her ratting her hair until it filled the room. He could almost feel sorry for the guy, but that didn't mean he could overlook the fact that Eibersen had thrown that punch. He sighed. "Any other episodes of violence?"

Camille picked up a hairbrush and began dragging it through her shoulder-length hair, smoothing and caressing. Jillian said, "He used to throw things, stomp around yelling and screaming."

"He threw a bowl of caviar on the kitchen floor," Geraldine said, no doubt considering it proof of insanity. "A crystal bowl."

"He drove his car up onto the sidewalk, knocked over some potted trees and crashed right into the barrier in front of the TV station," Jillian said quietly. "I was at the reception desk. I thought he was going to come right through the glass into the building."

No doubt about it, the guy definitely had a screw loose. Zach finished scribbling in his notebook, flipped it closed and dropped it into his pocket. "Okay. Here's the deal. I've heard enough to believe he can be dangerous, and you're a public personality, Ms. Waltham, which makes you even easier to get at than the average individual. So I propose we bring in a couple of subcontractors to keep an eye on you."

She turned away from the mirror then. "I can't have a couple of goons trailing me everywhere I go. What would people think?''

Zach just barely curbed the urge to roll his eyes. "I don't use 'goons,' as you put it. These men are professionals. They can keep a discreet distance. It won't be enough to completely protect you, so you'll have to be on your guard.''

Camille turned back to the mirror, her reflection laughing at him. "For Pete's sake, Keller, all I want you to do is stop the man from bothering me. He's not trying to kill anybody.''

"Not yet," Zach said. "But who can say he won't cross that line if he gets frustrated enough.''

She had coaxed her hair into a sleek flip. She smoothed it now with her hands, turning her head this way and that. "Jan was born frustrated,'' she said in a bored tone, "but he's not stupid. He won't do anything in front of witnesses, and since I'm never without an escort in public, I don't see what the problem is.''

Zach felt an instant of relief. He could just turn around and walk out now. He'd given her his take on the problem, and she'd rejected it. Nothing was keeping him here now—except a pair of big, sky-soft eyes clouded with worry. It occurred to him that if he washed his hands of Camille Waltham right here and now he could ask her sister out on a proper date, and just the thought of that kind of freedom scared him right back into Camille Waltham's corner.

"Is that tuxedo in there an example of the kind of escort you take out in public with you?'' he demanded.

It was Geraldine who came to the man's defense. "And just what's wrong with my ex-stepson?'' she asked in a mystified tone.

Zach smirked. "I'm sure he's from the very best of families, ma'am, but I doubt he could disarm a cranky toddler with a sucker, let alone a drunk with a grudge and a gun.''

The color bled right out of her face. "We don't know that Jan has a gun,'' she said weakly.

"We don't know that he doesn't.''

He gave that a few seconds to sink in before he went on, addressing himself to Camille this time. "Maybe we can compromise with protection in public only, provided you follow my instructions.''

"Listen to him, Camille," Jillian pleaded softly. "Please."

Camille rolled her eyes. "Oh, all right, if you're that scared of the harmless loser, I'll let the big, bad expert handle it."

Jillian seemed relieved, but Zach frowned. He didn't like being put down by a stuck-up little broad with more hair than sense, but he *really* didn't like watching her put down the sister who was so obviously concerned for her. Still, their interpersonal relationships were no business of his. His business was protecting the little witch, and he got down to it without further ado.

"Starting tomorrow," he said, "I'll want a list of your public appearances so I can have someone on hand to protect you. I'll need a photo of Eibersen to show them."

"I'll have my secretary take care of both," Camille said tersely.

"You should be safe at the office," Zach went on. "Security's usually pretty tight at television stations, but I'll check to be sure. How do you get to work?"

"The station provides a limo."

"Okay. I'll talk to the driver. Now about this house. I noticed a security system monitor in the front hall. Is it activated?"

Camille shook her head. "It was here when I bought the place. I don't know anything about it."

"Well, I do," Zach said. He took out his wallet and went through it until he found the card he wanted. Walking forward, he laid it on the corner of her dressing table. "Call that number and get the system activated."

She glanced at the card, picked it up and held it out to Jillian, who hurried forward and took it. Obviously Jillian would be deputized to take care of the details on the home front, so he addressed the next order to her.

"Call a locksmith and get the locks changed. Even if Eibersen never had his own key, the locks I've seen so far are more decoration than security. I want a dead bolt and chain on every outside door. Got that?"

Jillian nodded solemnly. He took another card from his shirt pocket and handed it over, knowing that it contained nothing but a ten digit number. "That's how you can reach me, anytime, anywhere, in case of an emergency. And I do mean an emergency." He turned back to Camille, brushing back the sides of his coat to settle his hands at his waist. "If you want to talk over arrangements or check on my progress, you call the office. Understand?"

Camille swiveled all the way around on her upholstered stool then. "What progress?" she asked.

"I'm going to do some investigating," he said, "see if I can locate Eibersen and figure out what he's up to. I should have a better handle on the situation in a few days. I like to know what I'm up against."

Camille sniffed at that. "You're up against a hapless boozer," she said dismissively.

"Maybe so," he said, "but all it takes to pull a trigger is a finger that works."

"You don't really think he'd try to kill her, do you?" Geraldine asked worriedly.

He gave her his most reassuring look. "I don't know, but until I do, I don't want her taking any chances. That clear?" He addressed that last to the room at large and got murmurs and nods. "Okay. Now, where's that window?"

"I'll show you," Jillian said, and he held out an arm, turning toward the door with her.

It was then that Camille Waltham finally remembered her manners. She came up off the tuffet and flitted across the room toward them, calling, "Oh, Mr. Keller." She stopped and smiled. "Zachary."

"'Zach,'" he responded, letting her know that he had no objection to the familiarity and that she had his attention.

She sparkled in a very deliberate manner and said, a little breathlessly, "Thank you. I appreciate you taking the time to handle this."

"You'll get a bill," he told her ungraciously, disliking the sparkle as much as the hauteur.

She turned on a brilliant smile. "Of course." She tugged on

the sash of her robe, letting it fall open as she switched her attention to her sister. "Send everyone in, Jilly. And tuck in that shirttail. You look like a rebellious teenager."

Zach was unmoved by the flash of compact curves that he got before she whirled away, so much so that he didn't even bother to react. Instead, he grabbed Jillian's hand, keeping her from tucking in that shirttail as she'd been instructed, and all but dragged her out of the room. Rebellious teenager, indeed. Somebody ought to take Camille down a peg or two, but it wouldn't be him. Nosirree, Bob. Not in this life. She wasn't *his* sister, after all. He found himself wanting to say something about it to Jillian, but he reminded himself that it wasn't any of his business. None whatsoever. And that was just the way he wanted it to stay.

They were halfway down the hallway before he realized that he was still holding her hand.

She kept expecting him to drop her hand at any moment, and yet when he did, she felt an unexpectedly intense disappointment. Or was that guilt? She hadn't expected to be quite so torn about telling him the whole story. Camille had only agreed to speak with him on the condition that Jillian go along with her version of events, and Jillian knew all too well that any deviation from the plan would bring down censure and blame on her head, from Camille as well as Gerry. Still, it seemed unfair to keep anything back. Not that it would make any difference in this case. Camille and Janzen had broken up, and he seemed bent on punishing Camille. Why, didn't really matter. Did it?

They reached the back door, and Jillian turned the knob unthinkingly. A wave of heat engulfed them as she pulled the door open, and as usual she couldn't help thinking that it had been a sizzling Texas summer that had driven her parents onto that sailboat off the coast of Galveston Island and to their deaths.

"Is the door always left open like this?" Zach asked incredulously, catching it as she stepped back to let it swing inside.

She stopped in her tracks. "Well, yeah, I guess so, whenever anyone's home, anyway."

He elbowed past her to examine the locking mechanism. "I

was right. This has to be replaced. Get a dead bolt and chain installed, too. And from now on keep it locked, bolted *and* chained whenever anyone's home.''

"All right."

He turned to examine the security system component mounted on the wall. "This is a dual system. You understand, don't you, that once it's activated you'll have to key in a security code every time you come in to keep the alarm from sounding?"

She hadn't actually, but she nodded anyway. "What, exactly, is a dual system?"

"It means there are two alarms, one here that's meant to scare off an intruder and warn the occupants, another to alert the police. This particular setup gives you about a minute and two tries to key in the code."

"I see."

He ushered her through the door and pulled it closed behind him. "Let's take a look at that window."

She led him away from the carport, across the patio and through the gate in the fence around the pool, then along the back of the house to the broken window. The double-wide window was set in the wall at about shoulder height. A board had been nailed over it, and broken glass littered the ground, none of the pieces larger than a man's hand. Zach went down on his haunches and gingerly stirred and studied the shards, some of them streaked and speckled with bright-red spray paint. After a few moments, he looked up at the three-letter word sprayed onto the brick.

"When did this happen?"

"Last night about 1:00 a.m."

"Did anyone hear or see anything?"

She nodded. "I was asleep in this room, and the shattering of the glass woke me up."

"This is your room?"

"Uh, no. It's, um, more private than my room sometimes, though."

He lifted an eyebrow at that but made no comment. "What happened after the window broke?"

"I called for Camille because the glass was all over the floor inside and I couldn't get to my slippers without cutting my feet. She phoned the police, but he was long gone by the time the call was made."

"But you're sure it was Eibersen?"

"Who else could it be?"

He didn't answer that, just stood and turned in a slow circle, surveying the area. He pointed back toward the pool gate. "He must have come from that direction. The fence is too tall on the other side, and I assume the pool gate is left open all the time?"

Jillian shrugged apologetically. "Yes, sorry."

"Get a chain and lock for it," he said dismissively. She nodded, adding that to her growing mental list. He turned back to the house, muttering, "Wonder why he chose this window. Why not Camille's bedroom window? I assume he knows which that would be."

Jillian felt the bottom drop out of her stomach, but she managed to keep her voice and tone level. "Oh, yes, he knows."

"Probably he was afraid of being seen through the larger windows," Zach mused. "What room *is* this room anyway?"

Jillian bit her lip. "Well, it's supposed to be a maid's room, but we don't have a live-in maid. Since my own room is right next to Camille's, I thought this one might be more private, but the broken window changed my mind about the desirability of that."

Zach nodded and made no further comment, and Jillian let herself relax again.

"Well, I guess that's it for now," he said, starting back the way they'd come. "You'll see to the locks and the security system?"

"Yes, first thing tomorrow."

"Good."

He led the way back across the pool yard and the patio, then held open the door beneath the carport as she passed through it into the hallway and blessed coolness. He followed her down the hall to the kitchen. It was her favorite room in the house, with its bright-yellow walls and clean white cabinets, stainless-steel appliances, pale, natural woods and terra cotta dishes. "Want another cool drink before you go?" she asked hopefully.

"Glass of water would be nice," he mumbled distractedly. He stood at the bar, arms folded and one hand rubbing his chin, obviously deep in thought, while she took down two glasses from the cabinet and filled them with ice water through the refrigerator door. She placed them on the bar and pulled out a stool, then perched on top of it.

"Have a seat."

Instead, he turned and leaned forward, bracing his upper body weight on both elbows. "It doesn't make sense that he chose to paint that particular window. I mean, it's behind the fence. Someone would have to go swimming in order to see it."

Jilly felt a hard knot form in the center of her chest. "Well, um, C-Camille swims every morning, year-round. The pool's heated." She didn't bother saying that she, too, liked to get in twenty or thirty laps before breakfast most mornings.

Zach nodded. "Okay. That kind of makes sense." Straightening, he picked up the glass left for him and drained it in one long gulp, the ice clinking and tinkling. "Ah-h-h. Nothing like a Texas summer to make you appreciate cold water."

"Funny you should mention that," Jillian said softly, her thoughts returning once more to her parents.

"Why's that?"

She stroked her fingertip through the condensation forming on the side of her glass. "Oh, it's just that my parents said something very like that before they left on the last impulsive jaunt that got them killed."

Zach swirled the ice in his glass thoughtfully. "I think you said that it was a boating accident?"

She nodded. "That's right. Dad always said that the Gulf of Mexico was a poor excuse for an ocean, but it was so hot that week, and it didn't seem worthwhile to fly all the way to the West Coast just for the weekend, so they flew to Houston, drove down to Galveston and rented a boat."

"And you never saw them again," he concluded.

She sighed. "The bodies were never even recovered."

He seemed to be searching for the right words to say, and finally came out with, "Man, that's tough. How old were you again?"

"Eleven."

He shook his head. "So young. How come you weren't with them?"

She smiled wanly. "I'm not much of a sailor. I like to swim, but boats do a number on my stomach, always have."

"That's certainly fortunate."

"It was hard to think of it that way at the time," Jillian said.

He nodded and murmured, "I can imagine." He shifted positions, signaling a shift in subject. "So you wound up here with your half sister and your father's ex-wife."

"Not here as in this same house, but yes, I wound up with Camille and Gerry."

"And no doubt you're grateful for that."

"Of course," she said lightly.

"Which is why you let her treat you like a lower life form," he said, almost offhandedly.

Jillian blinked in shock. "I beg your pardon!"

He grimaced and backed up a step, throwing up his hands. "I'm sorry. I shouldn't have said that."

She got to her feet. "You certainly shouldn't have! Camille does not treat me like..." Jillian bit her lip. "She's overprotective, is all. She still thinks I'm thirteen and mad at the world."

"Were you?" he asked. "Mad at the world, I mean."

She looked down, surprised to find that she was twisting her hands together. "Maybe," she said, but in truth she didn't remember it like that. She only remembered feeling lost and alone, a disappointment to those she loved most. Forcing her hands down to her sides, she said, "You don't understand Camille. Hers is a tough business, and she's learned to use arrogance as a shield against criticism. She's not really like that. In fact, sometimes I think she's really very insecure."

He lifted an eyebrow as if doubting the correctness of her assessment, but he merely remarked, "It really isn't any of my business. I apologize if I offended you."

"I just don't want you to think that Camille is a bad person," she told him softly.

"I can see that you love her very much," he said, as if that was all that mattered.

Jillian smiled. "She's my sister, and she gave me a home when no one else would or could."

"And that's very commendable," he said. A heartbeat later he added, "Well, I'd best be going. I have a dinner engagement. Thanks for the cold drink, or rather, drinks."

"I'll show you out," she said, moving away from the counter. Nodding, he followed her through the house to the front door.

"I didn't realize we were interfering with your social life," she said, even knowing that it was none of her business.

"Oh, it's no big deal," he assured her. "My brother and sister-in-law know only too well the demands of my business."

Jillian felt a flash of relief. It wasn't a date, then; rather, a family engagement. "Well, extend my apologies if we've made you late."

"Not necessary," he told her, pausing at the front door. "Don't forget, now, locksmith and security service, first thing tomorrow morning."

"I won't forget."

"I'll be in touch."

"Excellent." She opened the door for him, and he started out into the heat. "Oh, and, Zach, uh, Mr. Keller?"

He stopped and turned back. "Zach will do. What's up?"

"I just wanted to thank you."

He smiled and bowed slightly from the waist. The effect was absolutely dazzling. "All part of the service, ma'am." He winked and started off down the sidewalk, calling over his shoulder, "Later."

She watched him all the way to his car, a sporty, two-door model in black with a white convertible top. For once she didn't feel the heat—except on the inside. This time, it was all inside.

The shrill, familiar sound pierced the darkness of a deep, easy sleep. Zach jerked awake knowing exactly what that sound represented. On his stomach as usual, he levered up onto one elbow and reached for the cellular phone on his bedside table with the other hand. The antenna was up, and the phone within easy reach on an otherwise clean tabletop. Rolling over, Zach pushed the send button, clapped the tiny phone to the side of his head and cleared his throat. He'd had a busy couple of days and gotten to bed late after taking in a Friday-night movie with his older brother, Brett, and Brett's wife, Sharon, but his mind was clear as a bell.

"Keller here."

"He came into my house!" blurted a shrill voice. "He came right in while we were all sleeping and destroyed my kitchen!"

"Calm down and tell me who this is," he barked.

A shocked silence followed. "Well, who else would it be? Do you just go around handing out your emergency number on every street corner? You may be good-looking, Zach, but you're not very smart if that's how you do business."

Camille Waltham. Zach rubbed a hand over his face. He didn't bother to tell her that he had other clients. He doubted that it would penetrate that monumental ego. "Is anyone hurt?" he demanded.

He heard a huff, followed by, "Not really. He bumped into Jilly in the dark and knocked her down, but I don't think she's really hurt."

He was throwing back the covers before he even thought about doing it. "Have the police arrived?"

"I thought you were supposed to take care of things like this."

He caught the phone between his shoulder and his ear and reached for his jeans, then yanked them on. "We need documentation!" he snapped. "The police have their uses, too."

She started grumbling something about him not making himself clear, but he interrupted her. "I'll take care of it myself from here. Don't touch anything that he might have touched. Lock the doors and stay together. I'll be there as quickly as I can."

He hit the button, cutting her off before she could say anything else, then dropped onto the bed and grabbed for his socks. One of them went on inside out, but he couldn't have cared less. After picking up the phone again, he turned it on and punched in the police dispatch number. As he stomped into his boots and threw on a clean chambray shirt, he told the dispatcher where to send the patrol car, pocketed his wallet and grabbed his keys.

Clipping the phone to his waistband, he flew out of the apartment and down the hall to the elevator. Forty-five seconds later he was backing the convertible out of its parking space and heading down the garage ramp. Less than ten minutes passed before he pulled to a stop in front of the Waltham house. The police were already there and moving up the sidewalk. Fortunately he knew both officers.

"Jennings! Carpenter!"

Both stopped. "Hey, Keller," said the older man. "This one of yours?"

"Afraid so." He caught up to them and ushered them both up the walkway. "My client says the perp broke into the house and destroyed her kitchen."

"Is this the Camille Waltham who's on the news?" asked the younger man, Jennings.

"The same."

"She seems real nice," mused Jennings.

"Seems," Zach muttered, reaching for the doorbell.

The door opened almost immediately, revealing Gerry in pink silk and a white terry-cloth turban. Devoid of makeup, her face looked older and harsher. "It's about time!" she exclaimed. "We might have been murdered in our beds!"

Zach bit his tongue to keep from reminding her that only two days earlier she'd doubted very much that Janzen Eibersen meant harm to anyone. Instead, he pushed past her and into the house, motioning for the officers to follow him. "Where is everyone?"

"In the living room."

He walked into the room and found that *everyone* consisted of Camille in a pretty blue chiffon gown, her head in her hands. Alarm shot through him. "Where's Jillian?"

She looked up, her eyes going wide at the sight of his unbuttoned shirt. "In the kitchen, I think."

He turned around and left her without another word, motioning for one of the officers to take his place. Since Carpenter was already questioning Gerry, Jennings got the assignment. Zach hurried through the house. When he entered the kitchen, he barely noticed the garish red marring the yellow walls and white cabinets. His attention was taken, instead, by Jillian sitting at the bar in a big T-shirt, a damp, folded towel pressed to her face, her long legs and slender feet bare. Her hair was disheveled, wisping about her face like a feathery cap. Those abominable eyeglasses were nowhere in sight. She made him think of a fairy who had lost her wings.

"Jillian!"

She looked up at the sound of his voice, and a myriad of emotions roared through him at the sight of those big blue eyes and her battered face: rage, dismay, compassion, fear. Desire. Instinctively, he opened his arms, and with a small cry, she rushed into them. Her arms slid around his waist inside his open shirt, her bare skin against his igniting explosions along his nerve endings. He rocked backward, not because of the impact of her slender body, which was negligible, but because of the breathtaking effect of her unfettered breasts pressing against his chest with only a single layer of soft fabric between them.

He knew then that this battered imp of a female had somehow worked her way beneath his professional armor and his satisfying well-ordered existence had gone painfully awry.

Chapter Three

"Are you all right?"

Jillian nodded, sniffing. She seemed fragile and feminine in his arms, dangerously so. After a moment, he slid his hands to her shoulders and eased her away from him.

She smiled up at him, blue eyes glittering softly. "What is it?"

He had trouble forcing out the words, rage choking him. "Did he hit you?"

She shook her head, putting a hand to it as if the motion hurt her. "No."

He swallowed down the rage before steering her back toward the bar and lifting her up onto the stool there. She was as light as a feather. He picked up the cold, folded towel and held it gently to her cheek. "Tell me what happened."

She slid her hand over his, and he let her take the towel. Leaning on her elbow, she took a deep breath and told him everything. "I couldn't seem to sleep for some reason. About two, I heard someone here in the kitchen, and I thought it was Gerry, who sometimes has trouble sleeping, also. So, I got up and came out into the hall, thinking I'd offer to make us some warm milk or herb tea. It was dark. For some reason I didn't turn on the light in my room, but I expected to see the light from the kitchen. Still, I wasn't particularly frightened—until I heard the hissing.''

"The hissing?"

"I thought it was gas escaping from the stove," she said. "I ran down the hall to the kitchen, and that's when I saw the light."

"You said the light was off," he pointed out.

She nodded. "Yes, the kitchen light was off, but he had a flashlight."

"Eibersen?"

"I think so. I didn't actually see his face. He was dressed all in black and his hair was covered up."

Zach grimaced with disappointment. "Go on."

"Well," she said, "I screamed."

"And what happened then?"

She shrugged. "It all happened so fast. I think I must have scared him half to death, because he jumped about a foot, dropped the can and took off. He was scrambling like a madman, and he bumped into me. My foot kind of caught with his, and I went down, smacking my cheek on the other side of the bar there and landing on my shoulder." She laid down the cool towel and put her hand to her shoulder, wincing as she rotated the joint. "I grabbed at him," she went on, "and broke a fingernail." She held up her right hand, displaying an index finger with the nail torn back into the quick. "Before I could get to my feet again, he was gone. Camille came in and turned on the light. That's when we saw this." She waved a hand toward the cabinets, and for the first time Zach really looked around him.

"Holy cow!" he said, his jaw dropping as he took it all in. "The can he dropped was obviously a paint can."

"Spray paint seems to be his medium of choice," she commented wryly.

Zach was shaking his head, trying to make it all out as he read aloud. "This time my heart knows—"

"'Its mind,'" she supplied. "'This time my heart knows its mind. I am yours. You are mine.' It's from a poem."

"A poem?" he echoed incredulously.

Sighing, she recited the whole thing for him. It was a pretty sappy piece about finding true love after many false hopes and mistakes, only to be rejected. "'But I am constant,'" she recited, "'and will not be swayed. True love always finds a way.'"

Zach studied the sloppy letters dripping bright red on the walls, cabinets and appliances. "This guy is nuts," he decided finally. "I've been told that he's fixated, but this doesn't sound like he's punishing Camille. It sounds like he wants her back and thinks vandalism is a courtship technique!"

Jillian closed her eyes wearily. "I take it you haven't found him yet."

Zach pushed out a disgusted sigh and shook his head. "He seems to be moving around, one night in this motel, one night in another. From what I've gathered so far, he's sold or given away just about everything he owns."

"Isn't that what suicides do?" asked a worried voice from the doorway.

Zach turned to find Gerry and the others there.

"I don't have any indication that he's planning a suicide," he told her.

Camille pushed her way past her mother then, her nose turned up haughtily. "You don't have any indication of anything, from what I can tell! You haven't even found him yet!"

Zach rolled his eyes, holding on to his temper. "As I just told your sister, he's been moving around a lot, but we'll come across him sooner or later."

She waved a hand angrily at Jennings, who peered sheepishly over Gerry's white turban. "Just tell this idiot to go out and arrest him!"

Zach sent the man an apologetic look. "It isn't that simple, I'm afraid."

"I don't understand why not!"

"I didn't see his face, Camille," Jillian said, taking the blame. "I can't swear that it was him."

"And even if she could," Zach said irritably, "the cops don't know where to look for him."

"They would if you'd do your job!" Camille snapped.

"I'm doing my job!" he told her heatedly. "If you don't like the way I'm doing it hire someone else."

She folded her arms but said nothing more. He pushed a hand through his hair. "What I can't figure out is how he got past the security system." Camille looked away. Gerry suddenly got busy folding and smoothing the collar of her robe.

It was Jillian who cleared her throat and said, "The security system hasn't been activated."

Zach couldn't believe it. Throwing up both arms he bawled, "*What? You* told me you'd activate the system *that next day*."

"I tried," she said defensively. "But you have to choose a security code, and Camille—"

He whirled on Camille then. "I should have known! You just couldn't be bothered, I suppose!"

She drew herself up regally. "I am a very busy person, I'll have you know, and—"

"You egotistical little twit!" he yelled, and then he turned to Jillian once more. "What about the locks? You got those changed, didn't you?"

She gulped and bowed her head. "The locksmith was booked up. He's coming tomorrow afternoon."

"But he's the very best," Gerry added helpfully. "I believe in always going with the very best in the field. Why, he's installed locks for the Pipers, and everyone knows they have a priceless art collection, not to mention all those jewels."

Zach rolled his eyes back in his head and smacked the heels of his hands against his temples, suppressing the urge to do worse. "God help me," he groaned. "You three don't need a private cop—you need a keeper!"

Carpenter elbowed his way into the room then, asking Zach, "Want us to get a crew in to dust for prints?"

"Won't matter," Jillian muttered warily. "He was wearing gloves."

Zach targeted her with a narrow look. "You're certain?"

She nodded. "I told you, he was dressed all in black, head to toe. He was even wearing a hood and a mask. I saw his hand where he was holding the flashlight, and he was definitely wearing black gloves.''

Zach sighed. "Bag the paint can," he said to the police officer, suddenly weary. "Maybe we can trace the buy." Carpenter nodded and fished a rubber glove from one pocket and a plastic bag from another.

Jennings came forward as his partner bagged the can, saying reluctantly, "I, um, better get a formal statement from her." He pointed an ink pen at Jillian. Zach nodded reluctantly, hands at his hips. "Okay, but make it quick. She's been through enough already."

The man parked himself in front of Jillian, legs braced wide apart, notebook in one hand, ink pen in the other. She told her story all over again, answering questions along the way. It was over in fifteen minutes.

Afterward, Carpenter conferred with Zach. "We can post a drive-by every hour or so for the next twelve, if you want."

Zach rubbed a hand across his nape. That was exactly what he'd ask for under almost any other circumstances, but something wasn't right about this situation. "It's all right. I'll...I'll stay till morning." He sent a murderous glare at Camille and added, "At which point the security system will definitely be activated."

Camille flipped a shoulder unconcernedly. "What I want to know is who's going to take care of this mess?"

Jillian immediately volunteered. "I'll take care of it tomorrow."

"It really ought to be wiped down now," Gerry said.

"I want pictures of it first," Zach said. "Besides, Jillian isn't wiping down anything. She's been injured, in case you didn't notice."

Gerry seemed to think she'd been insulted. "Well, really!"

"Yes, really," Zach snapped.

Camille huffed in a put-upon way. "Are you all right, Jillian?" Jillian nodded. "I'm okay. You go on to bed."

"I *do* have an early call tomorrow," Camille said, "as usual."

"Just make yourself comfortable, young man," Gerry said, pattering after her retreating daughter.

"Sure," Zach drawled. "Thanks." Gerry didn't seem to even hear the sarcasm.

"I'll show you where to sleep," Jillian said softly.

"Never mind," he said, irritated at her behavior. "The couch will do me just fine. Right now I want to take a look at the point of entry. Do you have any idea where that might be?"

"Well," she said, "he went out the back door."

A muscle twitched in Zach's clamped jaw. He motioned to Carpenter. "You come with me. Jennings, have you got a camera in that squad car?"

"Sure do. I'll run get it."

"Wait here," he told Jillian. She nodded and pressed the cool towel to her cheek once more.

It didn't take long to determine that the lock had not been forced. They looked around for a few minutes but found nothing unexpected. By the time they were satisfied that there was nothing helpful to be found, Jennings had taken all the necessary photos of the damage done to the kitchen. Zach saw the police officers out and returned to Jillian. She looked unutterably weary.

"Well, whoever it was, he definitely has a key," Zach said.

"Yes, I'm sure he does," she admitted.

"But you're willing to wait for the Pipers' society locksmith," he said caustically. Then he pinched the bridge of his nose with thumb and forefinger, eyes closed, and tried to calm himself. "I'm sorry. I'm not mad at you. It's Camille's house and Camille's problem."

"Which I'm sure Camille will take much more seriously now."

He lifted an eyebrow at that but said only, "How're you feeling?"

She shrugged and winced. "Shoulder's tightening up, but otherwise—"

"Here," he said, stepping around behind her. "Let me have a look." He pulled down the soft neckline of her big shirt, exposing her shoulder blade. Sliding his fingers over her satiny skin, he gently probed, rotating the joint slightly. "I don't see any bruising," he said, mouth suddenly dry. "It's not out of joint."

"I didn't think it was," she whispered huskily.

The sound of her voice sent shivers up his spine. He jerked his hands away, saying, "Got any frozen peas?" The question came out strangled.

"What?"

He cleared his throat. "Frozen peas. They make a great ice pack."

"Oh. Probably in the freezer."

She started to slide off the stool, but he held up a hand to stop her. He went over to the double-wide freezer-refrigerator in the corner, opened the door on the left and rummaged around the bins, finding what he needed. "Frozen corn works just as well," he said, carrying the bag over to the counter. He started pulling open drawers until he found another towel. He carried the towel and the bag of frozen corn back to the bar. Folding the bag inside the towel, he fashioned a sling to hold the "ice pack" in place by looping the towel under her arm and tying it around her shoulder. "Now, let me see that finger."

She held up her right index finger. "It's no big deal."

He surveyed it briefly. "Where's the peroxide?"

"Uh, there's a first-aid kit in the cabinet above the sink."

He went there, used a paper towel to open the messy door and took down the kit, then carried it back to the bar counter. He fished around inside, extracting Band-Aids, antibiotic cream and a small pair of scissors. Using the scissors, he clipped the nail neatly. Then he applied the cream and two Band-Aids, one over the end of her finger and the other wrapping around it. "That ought to do it," he said.

She thanked him timidly, adding, "You don't have to take care of me, you know."

He pulled out the other stool and sat down, knowing perfectly well that he ought to keep his mouth shut, but somehow, he just couldn't. "Someone has to," he said. "Your sister obviously won't."

Jillian couldn't quite seem to look him in the eye. "It wouldn't occur to her. You have to understand how busy she is."

"I understand that she dumps everything that doesn't have to do with her precious career on you."

She didn't even argue with him. "I don't mind," she said. "I like doing things around the house."

He wanted to shake her, to make her stand up for herself, but it wasn't any of his business. Why, he wondered, did the sweet ones always get treated like this? Suddenly he realized what he was thinking, and was shocked at himself. It must have shown, for she laid a hand on his forearm and asked earnestly, "What is it?"

He didn't want to talk about it. He really didn't, and yet… "You remind me of someone I used to know," he finally said.

"Oh? And who would that be?"

He shifted uncomfortably. "We're getting off the subject. We were talking about how you let certain people take advantage of you and then put you down, when they ought to be grateful and supportive."

She smiled wryly, as if touched by his concern. "It's not like that. I'll admit that it hasn't always been easy, but it's more Gerry than it is Camille, and before you start in on her, just think about it from her viewpoint. She was replaced, literally, by my mom, who was several years younger, and yet she still took me in when I had no place else to go. It's natural that she should resent me, don't you think?"

"Maybe," he admitted, "but that was a long time ago. It doesn't explain this subservient role they've cast you in."

Jillian seemed to be searching for the right words to explain. "I know this sounds absurd, but it's almost as if Gerry is jealous of me on Camille's behalf. I can't imagine why, though."

"Oh, please," he said scathingly. "Your sister has the personality of a diva."

Jillian sighed. "I guess you're right," she admitted, "but she still has more personality than me, not to mention looks."

He could have let it pass. He should have let it pass. Instead, he said, "There's nothing wrong with your personality or your looks. You have those enormous blue eyes and that model's build going for you.''

Her mouth fell open, but then she laughed, sputtering chuckles.

"Stop that!" he ordered, angered that she'd take his compliment so lightly.

She sobered, biting her lip. "Sorry. It's just that tall and skinny does not a model make."

"Is that so?" he demanded. "Well, let me tell you something, lady. I happen to know a model's physique when I see one." Oh, brother! Why was he doing this? He meant to stop there, but the compulsion was too great. "Ever hear of Serena Gilbert?" he heard himself asking.

The name seemed to float around in her brain and finally make a connection. "Wasn't she that model who was killed by an obsessed fan?"

He nodded solemnly. "The same."

She gasped. "Oh, no! You were working for her, weren't you? You poor guy. You must've felt—"

"I wasn't working for her," he interrupted sharply. "But she's the reason I'm working for you, er, Camille, that is."

"What do you mean?"

He studied her face, wondering how best to get himself out of this, but in the end he found nothing with which to reply except the truth. He shrugged, trying to make light of it. "I was in love with Serena."

Her eyes widened and filled with tears. "Oh, Zach."

Suddenly he was almost enjoying himself, soaking up her pity like a sponge. "I was a policeman back then," he explained. "I trusted the system to take care of her stalker, but he still got to her, and that's when I realized I could do more good working the system from the outside instead of being a part of it."

"That's why you do what you do, why you work so often for free when your clients can't afford to pay."

He frowned. "Who told you that?"

She smiled. "Lois."

Of course. Lois was one of those who had been living hand-to-mouth while hiding from a controlling, abusive husband. He'd taken care of the husband and given her a job. She was the perfect secretary, except for a tendency to gossip. She seemed to think that bragging about him was part of the job description, no matter what he said. For once, he couldn't quite seem to be irritated about it.

"The cops have their hands tied in too many ways," he told Jillian sternly. "I promised myself that what happened to Serena wouldn't happen to anybody else on my watch, and so far it hasn't."

She laid a hand on his shoulder, her big blue eyes as soft as clouds. "I'm so sorry. I had no idea."

He fought down a smile and tapped her nose with the tip of one finger. "I just wanted to prove that I know what I'm talking about. You're not 'tall and skinny.' You're sleek and—unique, with that gamin face. And I'm quite sure I'm not the only one who has noticed."

Her smile was wide and bright. Pleased, he curled a finger under her chin and raised her face, realizing with a jolt that he'd intended to kiss her and had just barely avoided it. "Uh, I—I better have another look at this face."

She lowered the towel. He tenderly explored the bruised cheekbone, his fingers trembling with the effort not to hurt her. "Don't think anything's broken."

"I'm sure it's not," she agreed, her voice gone husky and soft.

He made himself look away, spied the first-aid kit and all but pounced on it. He searched around inside until he found a topical anesthetic. After uncapping the tiny atomizer, he sprayed some on his fingertips, then gently but liberally swabbed the painkiller on her cheek. "Does this hurt?"

She licked her lips, whispering, "No."

He literally could not keep his gaze from dropping to her mouth. Of their own volition, his fingertips feathered along the edges of her jaws. She closed her eyes, and he couldn't have stopped himself then if he'd wanted to. He kissed her, gently settling his mouth over hers, testing the fit and finding it perfect. She moaned and turned her head slightly. He remembered the way she'd felt in his arms, the free weight of her breasts pressed against him, and he pushed his hands into her hair. Silk. Caramel silk. Would she let him make love to her? he wondered, and just the fact that he did so, shocked him to the core. Dropping his hands, he jerked away. She looked as stunned as he felt. He gulped, inane words tumbling from his mouth. "My, uh, mom always says it's the kiss that makes it better."

She nodded dreamily. It took all his willpower not to reach for her again. Instead, he got up off the stool and began putting the first-aid kit back together.

"You'd better be getting to bed."

She nodded but otherwise didn't move.

"Some rest will do that shoulder a world of good," he went on.

She blinked and got down off the stool, reaching for the first-aid kit. "I'll, um, put this away," she murmured, but he moved it out of her way.

"I'll do this. You go on to bed."

"All right. Um, are you sure you wouldn't prefer that I show you to the extra room first?"

He shook his head. "Nah, I'll be perfectly fine on the couch in the den."

She put a hand to her head as if trying to think, and he was flattered despite himself. At least he knew that kiss had affected her as much as it had him. "If you need a blanket—" she began.

"No blanket, no pillow. I'll be fine. Take yourself off to bed, and if you hear a noise again, scream first, okay? No more wandering around in the dark. I'm here now, and when I'm not, you wait for the cops. You *don't* investigate. Understood?"

She smiled almost secretively. "Understood."

"Good." He winked and jerked a head toward the hall. "And good night."

"Good night."

She moved around the bar and started off down the hallway toward her room. Then she came back again and slipped off the sling. She laid the towel out on the counter, unfolded it and removed the bag of corn, which she then returned to the freezer.

"Maybe you'd better take an aspirin," he said.

"I have some in my bathroom," she told him shyly.

He stood at the end of the counter, watching as she moved down the hallway again. She paused and trilled him a little wave. He smiled, feeling absurdly giddy, and she ducked her head and went into her room. He put away the first-aid kit and switched off the overhead light. For a long moment he stood there in the darkness, contemplating that kiss.

He couldn't for the life of him imagine why he'd given in to the impulse, yet he couldn't quite be sorry about it, either. It had been, well, *right,* somehow. But it wouldn't happen again. He'd be on his guard next time. He had to be. He didn't want her to think that he was *interested* in her. It was against his policy, after all. Sort of. Not that it mattered. He had to keep his hands off her for lots of reasons. If he couldn't think of any right now, it didn't matter. They would come to him later. What mattered was that he must not kiss her again. It shouldn't be a problem. She wouldn't always look so vulnerable and softly needy as she had tonight. She wouldn't always need a shoulder to lean on or a strong arm to hold her.

He remembered how light and utterly feminine she had felt in his arms. She'd looked so fragile and ethereal sitting there with her bruised face, and he'd been ready to fight hordes of felons for her, to make the world pay for allowing her to be wounded. That was what had made him think of Serena. Sweet, gentle, unassuming Serena, so beautiful she hadn't seemed real, so sweetly vulnerable and giving. Yes, that was it, not the looks, because in truth they didn't look much alike. Perhaps they were built alike, but he always went for the long, lean type. Since Serena, though, he'd managed to keep his distance, and he could keep his distance this time, too. He had to, and so he would. From now on. Absolutely.

He hoped.

Jillian pulled the covers up to her chest, folded them back neatly and laced her fingers together over the fold. Sighing deeply, she closed her eyes once more. But it was no use. She couldn't sleep. Somehow, she wasn't even tired, which was funny because she'd been exhausted earlier. Then he had kissed her. He had really kissed her, and it had, somehow, made everything all right, just as he'd said. She pressed trembling fingertips to her lips, amazed and bemused all over again.

Why had he kissed her? Could he really be attracted to her? Or had he just felt sorry for her? He had said that she was "sleek and unique." Did he really think that? Should she believe him? *I know a model's physique when I see one. Gamin face. Enormous blue eyes. Model's build.*

And he had kissed her. Maybe she would believe him. Oh, it wasn't really her; she understood that.

You remind me of someone. Serena Gilbert. I was in love with her.

Still, he had kissed her, Jillian. That meant he was attracted to her. Didn't it? Even if he didn't like her, he was attracted to her. That was something. Wasn't it?

Sleek and unique.

That was something with which she could work.

She sat up suddenly and threw back the covers. After crawling over the end of the bed, she came to her feet and padded silently to the closet door. She pulled it open, switched on the light and looked into the mirror mounted on the door. Gathering the fabric of her T-shirt gown into her hands, she pulled it tight and studied her shape. She wasn't hopeless. She was…sleek and unique. Her breasts were small, but they were high and firm. Her waist dipped in rather nicely. She turned and cast a critical look over her shoulder. She didn't have much rear end, but at least her thighs weren't heavy. Turning again, she stepped closer and took a good look at her face. Her chin was entirely too pointy, and she hated the fact that her eyes took up half her face, but he seemed to like her eyes, and her mouth was good, the mouth he'd kissed. Her nose was too small for her face, but with her eyes crowding out everything else, she supposed it didn't matter much. Okay, so she wasn't beautiful, but she was attractive in her own way. She must be because he had kissed her.

Yes, she was definitely going to believe him.

Smiling, she pulled at the wisps of hair around her face, fashioning them this way and that until she was satisfied. Reaching into her closet, she pulled out first one garment and then another, rejecting most with a wrinkle of her nose. These were the clothes that Camille had picked for her, tailored, subdued, almost sexless. Jillian had worn them because it was easier to give in to Camille than to assert herself, but she knew that she wasn't going to do that anymore. She was sleek and unique; she was going to dress like it from now on. When she'd separated everything that did not appeal to her from that which did, she had precious little left, but some of the things still had the tags attached. She'd bought them on whimsy and then never found the courage or occasion to wear them. But no more.

Smiling, she switched off the closet light and closed the door. After crawling back into bed, she collapsed upon her pillow, thinking that it was time that the real Jillian Waltham stepped out into the light of day and demanded a little respect. Maybe the next time he kissed her, it would be because he was attracted only to her and not because she reminded him of someone he had loved. Maybe.

Maybe...

She awoke to laughter, and even before she glanced at the clock on her bedside table, she realized that she'd slept later than usual. Was he still here? A second burst of laughter told her that some male was definitely in the kitchen laughing with her sister. Throwing off the covers, she leaped to her feet and literally ran to the bathroom.

She took a quick—very quick—shower, shaving her legs with one hand and shampooing her hair with the other, then hurried to the closet and slapped through those things she'd set aside last night. Her hand fell on a black, sleeveless cotton knit dress with a neckline so wide that it slipped off one shoulder. For once, she decided to follow her first inclination and not second-guess herself. After slipping into black silk panties and a white tank top with spaghetti straps, she towel-dried her hair, then pulled on the dress. She dug out a pair of white leather sandals set with amber stones, and a narrow copper belt that looped loosely around her waist and dipped gently over one hip.

Impatiently, she blew her hair dry. Well, almost dry. Then finished it up by pulling and plucking it into wisps about her face and setting it with a few spritzes of hair spray from a pump dispenser. She grabbed her glasses from the bedside table by sheer rote and pushed them onto her face, only to stop as she caught sight of herself in the mirror above her dresser. Did he really like her big eyes? For once she was tempted not to hide them behind her glasses. She hadn't had the prescription changed in years, and she supposed that by most standards she didn't really need them, but they were almost a part of her, she'd worn them so long. She chewed her lip in indecision, then finally realized that if she was to maintain the spirit of the moment, she would have to follow her inclination. By way of compromise, she lifted the glasses off her face and carefully set them atop her head. She actually liked the effect. Except for the bruise on her cheek, she had never looked better. She decided to try a little camouflage, and stroked on a little powdered blush. More laughter spurred her to end her cosmetic application there and hurry out into the hallway.

Camille, Gerry and Zach were sitting at the bar in the kitchen, drinking coffee. Zach was the first to notice her. His surprised gaze took her in with one sweep, and he lifted both brows appreciatively. She couldn't possibly look as good as he did, though, with that dark morning beard shadowing his jaws and chin, his dark hair tousled charmingly.

"You slept well, I see."

She smiled, more pleased than if he'd told her she was beautiful, which she wouldn't have believed, but to look well, after the night she'd had, that was something. "Thank you."

"That dress is all wrong, though," Gerry said sourly. "I think it must be too big for you."

"Oh, I think it's made that way," Zach said lightly.

His green eyes danced merrily at Jillian as she crossed over to the cabinet, opened one of the ruined doors and took down a coffee cup. She poured herself a cup from the pot, uncertain what she was getting. Neither Gerry nor Camille could make a decent pot of the stuff. She took a sip and, to her surprise, found it to be quite good.

"Who made the coffee?"

Camille answered her. "Zach did. I tried my hand at it first—with the usual results."

"Meaning that I thought she was trying to poison me," Zach said teasingly.

Camille laughed, but Gerry frowned. "Camille is not a housemaid. She's a professional woman."

"True," Camille said, taking one final salute with her cup, "which means that I'd better get moving." She got down off her stool, saying, "Thanks for the coffee, Zach, and again, I apologize for my behavior last night. It was just the shock."

"No problem," Zach replied tersely.

"Zach wouldn't have had to make the coffee," Gerry noted, glaring at Jillian, "if you hadn't slept so long."

Camille rolled her eyes at that but said nothing, just wiggled her eyebrows at Jillian as she moved past her. Jillian wasn't certain what the message was. Perhaps Camille was complimenting her on her looks, or perhaps she was indicating that Gerry had bats in the belfry. Or maybe she was saying that Zach Keller was worth making apologies to and dressing for. Jillian felt a pang of intense jealousy over that laughter earlier, but the next instant guilt swamped her. She had no right to jealousy. A simple kiss didn't entitle her to possessiveness. She should be glad that Camille and Zach seemed to have made peace. Camille's safety could well depend on it. She made herself smile and go to the pantry for bagels.

"We have bagels with cream cheese or butter and jam. Anyone interested?"

"None for me," Camille called as she moved down the hallway.

"I'll take cream cheese," Zach said heartily as she opened the refrigerator.

She took out not only the cream cheese but also a container of sliced cantaloupe and strawberries.

"It's nonfat. Hope you don't mind," she told Zach.

"Not in the least."

"We have cottage cheese, Gerry, if you'd rather have it."

Gerry sniffed. "No, thank you."

"Zach?"

"Not for me."

Jillian closed the refrigerator door and began slicing bagels for the toaster. She popped them in, four halves at once, and depressed the slide. As she took down plates from the cabinet, Gerry said nastily, "I see you're not wearing a bra today."

Jillian momentarily froze, but then she smiled and carried the plates to the bar. Zach's gaze was direct and slightly challenging. She merely passed him a plate. She knew perfectly well that defending herself to Gerry would only exacerbate the problem. Unfortunately, Gerry's venom was not spent.

"I don't approve of going without one's bra," she went on conversationally. "Not only is it indecent, it makes one's breasts droop unflatteringly."

Jillian almost grinned. It was such absurd breakfast table conversation! Zach seemed to think so, too. His eyes were brimming with laughter, but his face was perfectly solemn when he turned to Gerry and said, "Decency, they tell me, is like beauty. It's in the eye of the beholder. Personally, I don't usually give much thought to what other people wear under their clothing. You might be right about the drooping, though. But then, how do you explain all those models who go around without bras all the time? They don't seem to droop. Maybe that's why some men, myself included, tend to prefer women with small, firm breasts."

Gerry's mouth was hanging open. It was perfectly all right for her to speak inappropriately to make a point, but the idea that Zach should speak so frankly about such a delicate subject clearly shocked her. Jillian bit her lip to keep giggles from sputtering out of her mouth.

Gerry said, in her most haughty tone, "I wasn't trying to spark debate, young man. I was merely trying to help the girl."

Zach grinned at Jillian and winked. "I don't think she needs your help in this instance. She's got that model's build going for her." His gaze targeted her bust, and he concluded, "No drooping there."

Gerry sounded as if she were strangling. Jillian felt her face begin to burn, but she was flattered, too, inordinately so. She mouthed a silent, "Thank you."

Gerry's heightened color seemed to come from another source entirely. Jillian had seen her enraged before but never trying to swallow it like this. Zach must have sensed the building tension, but he gave no evidence of it as she delivered the toasted bagel to his plate and offered him the cheese with a case knife stuck in it.

"Thanks," he said companionably, spreading cream cheese on his bagel. She took out forks, one for each of them and another to serve the fruit. "So," he said, "did you sleep as well as you look like you slept?"

She laughed. She just couldn't help it. "Yes, I did. Thank you. How about you?"

He scratched at the dark stubble on his cheek. "Probably."

"Well, you must have slept just fine, then," she told him brightly, surprised to find herself flirting.

He beamed a blinding smile at her. "You know," he said, "I think I'm just now seeing you as yourself. Before you were either uniformed—" She made a face, and he laughed. "Yeah, pretty ghastly—or, I don't know, just not yourself. Although, the middle-of-the-night-emergency-wear wasn't bad."

Jillian laughed again. Gerry got up and left the room in a huff, muttering something about having to talk to Camille. Zach seemed no more disturbed by her leave-taking than Jillian was.

"How's the shoulder?" he asked, reaching for the fruit.

"It's fine. Everything's fine."

"You look it," he said softly. Then he picked up his bagel and bit into it. She followed suit, and they passed several minutes in companionable silence. It was a wonderful way to start the day. Even with the cabinets and walls splattered with grotesque red and her small aches and pains to remind her of the night's misadventure, she had never felt quite so lighthearted. Zach Keller was good for her state of mind, it seemed. She couldn't help wondering if he'd be as good for her heart.

Chapter Four

Zach was just a bite away from finishing his bagel when Camille breezed into the room wearing a royal-blue suit with a melon-colored blouse and a striped scarf folded ascot-style beneath the open collar. She carried a briefcase in one hand and a garment bag in the other. Her blond hair had been coiled into a sleek, prim roll on the back of her head.

"I have just enough time for a bite of that fruit," she announced, and Jillian instantly got up to get her a plate.

"The sight of this kitchen makes me sick every time I see it again," Camille complained, divesting herself of her baggage in order to reclaim her seat at the bar and be waited upon. "Get someone over here to clean it up today, Jilly. I can't bear to look at this mess."

"But it's Saturday," Jillian said quietly, placing a small plate of fruit, a fork and a napkin, along with a fresh cup of coffee, in front of her sister. Camille went to work on it without a word of thanks.

"I don't see what that's got to do with anything. People work on Saturdays."

"Some do," Jillian agreed quietly, "but I have the studio today, if you recall."

"Oh, that." Camille shrugged. "You can putter around there another time."

"What studio is this?" Zach asked, unable to keep silent in the face of Camille's obvious disdain.

"A friend and I share work space in her loft in Deep Ellum," Jillian said. "Since I work a regular job during the week, I get to the studio only on weekends."

Interested, Zach leaned forward, elbows on the countertop. "And what do you do in this studio?"

Camille waved her fork, saying peremptorily, "Jilly is a sculptor."

Zach was surprised and pleased. "Oh, really?"

"I have a degree in art," she divulged shyly, "with emphasis in sculpture."

"Which is why she makes sandwiches for a living," Camille said with a chuckle.

Jilly lifted her chin. "I do have a commission now," she said.

"That's great!" Zach said, tickled for her, perhaps more so than he ought to be.

Camille gulped down a bite of cantaloupe in order to say, "It's just a showing. She's not actually getting paid."

Zach wanted to kick Camille, but to his surprise, Jillian smiled and calmly explained, "It's going to be displayed in Deep Ellum, for sale, and if...*when* it sells, I'll be able to buy materials for several more pieces to go on display. It's really a neat concept. It's called the Art Bar, and it's sort of a combination gallery and club. Eventually I hope to have eight or nine works on display at all times. My friend Denise is contributing paintings, and we have some glass and pottery and other things coming in."

"Sounds exciting," Zach said, impressed.

"Sounds hopeless to me," Camille commented. "The kind of patrons that Deep Ellum draws is a party crowd, not an artsy crowd."

"I'm part of the Deep Ellum crowd," Jillian said, just a hint of defiance in her tone.

"Me, too," Zach said, though in truth his activity in Deep Ellum was limited to driving through it and sitting stakeout on a particular corner.

"That's two," Camille said mockingly.

Irritated, Zach decided it was time to put Miss Camille to some useful purpose. Retrieving his cell phone from his belt, he punched in a number from the memory menu, hoping he could catch his friend before he left the house. The brusque answer that cut off the sound of the telephone ringing told him that he had just managed to do so.

"Hey, Del. I know you're on your way out, buddy, so I won't keep you. Need a favor." He went on to explain that a client of his had called Del's company a few days earlier to have her home security system activated but had failed to decide on an access code, and as a result he'd found it necessary to spend the night keeping guard. "I need it settled before I leave here, so I thought I'd give the code to you and have you see to it personally first thing this morning. Does that work for you?" Before Del could answer him, a horn honked and Camille hopped down off the stool.

"That's my car. Gotta go!"

"Whoa!" Zach grabbed her by the wrist, twisting around on his stool in order to do it. "Code. Now."

She shook free of him. "I've got to go!"

"It's five digits, for Pete's sake! Either you choose them or I will! Now, do you want to be able to get into the house when you come back or shall I alert the police to expect a false alarm? It's a fining offense, by the way."

Camille groaned in exasperation and mentally began ticking numbers off on her fingers. Finally, she stomped one foot in frustration and exclaimed, "Seven one seven...seven four!"

Releasing her, Zach repeated the numbers into the telephone. Camille shot a loaded glance at Jillian, grabbed her things and rushed from the room. Zach gave Del the necessary information to activate the security system, thanked him and hung up. "Pays to know the right people," he said to Jillian.

"I suppose it does," she agreed, smiling wanly.

He sat there a few seconds longer, fighting the urge to ask her about her sculpting and wondering what that parting look had been about. Camille, no doubt, blamed Jillian for the two-minute delay needed to pick and communicate the code. Well, he was detecting stirrings of growing self-respect in Jillian this morning, and, oddly enough, it made him proud. When she started cleaning up their light breakfast, it occurred to him that he had no reason to linger.

"Guess I'll be going. Thanks for breakfast."

"I think it was the least we could do, don't you?" she replied, stacking plates.

"I get paid for this," he reminded her.

"But you wouldn't have to be paid if we had done what we were supposed to."

"More importantly you wouldn't have that bruise on your cheek."

"True."

She carried the plates to the counter, rinsed them and stacked them in the sink. He kept sitting there, admiring that little dress and wondering why he didn't just get up and go. Unbidden, the memory of her breasts, free beneath her nightshirt, pressing against his chest, came to him. He cleared his throat and started to get up. Gerry came flip-flopping down the hall then in her terry-cloth scuffs. Her turban had been replaced by a sleek blond hairstyle that made it clear to Zach that she wore a wig.

"Oh, Jilly," she called as she came, "I forgot to tell you that I need the car today."

"But it's Saturday!" Jilly exclaimed. "You know I have the studio on Saturdays."

"Oh, please," Gerry scoffed. "I have a friend in the hospital. Which is more important—that or you pretending to sculpt?"

"I don't pretend to do anything," Jillian said quietly, "but I guess I can take the bus."

"Just so," Gerry confirmed, pouring herself another cup of coffee.

Jillian sighed and moved to wipe down the bar top with a

sponge and some spray. Zach heard himself say, "I'll give you a lift."

She looked up as if shocked to find that he was still there. He was pretty shocked to find that, too. "You don't have to drive me around," she said, but even as she said it, her face lit up.

Unexpected words just kept coming out of his mouth. "No problem. I wouldn't have offered if it was a problem. I don't often get a chance to escort a real artist."

She laughed, her face positively beaming.

"She'll just have to take the bus back," Gerry pointed out sourly.

"Maybe not," Zach heard himself saying.

"I don't mind," Jillian said at the same time.

Zach shrugged, and Jillian added, "Just give me a minute to make a phone call, okay? If I don't at least try to get this place cleaned up, Camille will fry me."

Zach shook his head. Camille's safety was threatened, but the cabinets were a higher priority than activating the home security system. He'd never figure that one. As Jillian disappeared into another part of the house, he prepared himself to wait. After spending a few minutes explaining to Gerry how to activate the security system when she left the house, he poured himself another cup of coffee. She flopped off to finish dressing, and he settled down at the bar, but he'd barely cooled his coffee enough to start drinking it when she returned, a little white leather purse with a long chain slung over one shoulder.

"All done?"

"Umm-hmm. He'll come on Tuesday and take a look."

"I think most of it will just wash off," Zach said, pushing aside his cup.

Jillian held a finger to her lips. "Shhhh."

"What?" he whispered conspiratorially. "You don't want to spend your weekend scrubbing walls and cabinets?"

"I probably will anyway," she replied, wrinkling her nose, "but not today." Grinning, she grabbed his hand and ran with it the end of the counter, spinning him around on his stool. He hopped to his feet and let her pull him toward the front of the house. As they hurried through the rooms, his spirits seemed to lift incrementally for no reason whatsoever. Jillian herself seemed ebullient, so much so that they were both laughing by the time they hit the front door.

"Let's put the top down," she said eagerly as he let her into the passenger seat of his car.

"Absolutely." He ran around to the driver's side and let himself in, then snatched his sunshades from the visor overhead. Seconds later they were driving down the street, just a little too fast to be strictly legal, the wind blowing through their hair. When she reached up to pull down her glasses, he noticed that the lenses were the kind that turned dark in bright light. They made better sunglasses than regular glasses, and she looked absolutely charming with her butterscotch hair whipping in the wind. He punched on the radio, and vintage rock competed with the rush of the wind for supremacy. She leaned forward and turned up the volume. When she started to sing along in a surprisingly husky contralto, Zach put his head back and laughed, feeling young and impulsive and way, way cool.

Too soon they were pulling up to the curb in the funky eastside neighborhood known as Deep Ellum. The loft turned out to be one of several on the top floor of an old hat factory. He switched off the music and smiled at her. "Guess I'll see you later."

She nodded, then bowed her head. "Would you like to come up? Denise and Worly won't mind."

"What's a Worly?" he asked, laughing.

"That's Denise's husband. He's a musician."

"Why am I not surprised?"

"The Art Bar was Worly's idea," she said. "He talked the club owner into it."

"An enterprising musician. Now I am surprised."

She laughed. "Come on up. I'll show you what I'm working on."

He knew that he shouldn't. He'd spent too much time with her already. "I'd like to," he said, "but I have work to do. After last night, I really have to get on Eibersen's trail."

"Oh. Right," she said. She smiled, but her disappointment was palpable. "Well, thanks for the lift. I really appreciate it." She reached for the door handle, and he found himself reaching for the ignition.

"Heck, I can spare a few minutes. Besides, the curiosity is killing me."

Laughing, she sat back and waited until the top electrically descended, then she helped him latch it into place. She hopped out, and he locked the doors. As they walked up the sidewalk he used the remote to turn on the alarm. They stepped into a small foyer at the front of the building and climbed the metal stairs.

Zach took inordinate interest in the old light fixtures dangling overhead. It was either that or watch the sway of Jilly's slender hips and those long bare legs as she climbed the stairs. By the time they reached the top, his heart was beating much too hard. Jilly turned left and stopped before a shocking orange door bearing the life-sized painting of an angel in blue jeans who bore a striking resemblance to Jilly herself with long, pale-blond hair. Extracting a key from her purse, she unlocked the door and opened it. The room beyond was a shambles of stained furniture, dusty rugs and musical instruments, lit by the harsh sunshine pouring through a wall of bare, grimy windows.

"This way."

Jillian led him through the maze of instruments, furniture and amplifiers. The walls, he noticed were painted with a jumble of forest and jungle scenes where butterflies sported the heads of tigers and tigers the heads of humans. They passed through a small kitchen piled with empty pizza boxes and rows of neatly arranged empty beer bottles to a small, glassed-in room beyond. Paintings in various sizes and stages of completion were stacked haphazardly around the floor and on easels. Paints in every conceivable type of container, from half-gallon cans to fruit jars, were scattered over every surface, including the long, narrow table standing dead center of the clutter. Beneath the table was a contraption that looked like a boxed fan slanted over the top of a wooden box. Oddly, the fan seemed to blow *into* the box.

He barely had time to consider the purpose of that, however, for his attention was immediately captured by what sat atop the table.

It was a chunk of pale stone about sixteen inches tall and nine to ten inches across. Most of the outside of it was rough and natural, just as it must have come out of the ground, but one side had been cut away as the artist had carved her way inside the stone, fashioning an intricate vale of roots and warrens filled with a tiny world of mushroomlike villages.

"Holy cow!" he breathed.

"Actually, I call it *Treasure*," she said.

An apt title, he decided. He couldn't quite believe what he was seeing. He was still studying it, finding new bits in which to delight, when she moved on to another piece, this one only about the size of his fist. She picked it up and handed it to him. He was shocked at how light it felt as he turned it over in his hand. A little study revealed a sort of gnome emerging from the rock. He didn't have time to see more as she handed him yet another piece and another. He realized belatedly that she was speaking.

"All part of my fantasy period," she concluded, and moved on down the table. The pieces she handed him now were heavier and smoother. "I'd like to cast these in bronze," she said as he studied the graceful arch of one piece and the intricate swirl of another. He came to a piece of reddish stone striated with blond streaks that might have been a three-petaled flower not yet opened to the sun, a kind of tulip maybe, and yet not a tulip at all.

"What do you call this one?"

"*Trinity*," she said.

He lifted and turned it, watching the three "petals" swirl and flow into one. "It's a religious piece?" he asked.

"You could say that." She pulled a covering from a larger piece and leaned forward on both palms, studying it with a frown. "This is the new piece."

With a small shock of recognition, he noted the power tools surrounding it but the sculpture itself pulled too strongly at him to allow him time for reflection. It was a shape, nothing more, emerging from a hard, almost crystalline gray-blue stone that literally beckoned his hand. He reached for it, pausing at the last moment. "May I?"

"Absolutely."

He ran his hand over it, feeling the contrast of polished smoothness and rough cuts. "What is it?"

"I don't know. It'll tell me before long."

He was completely captivated, totally enthralled, so much so that he didn't notice the approach of another person until she drawled, "Good God, it's a man!"

He looked up, both hands on the stone, to find a freckle-faced woman with long, wildly curly red hair standing out at odd angles around her head and shoulders. Her eyes were a dark, chocolate brown. Her perfect oval face and shocking hair neatly offset the heavily muscled, squat body gloved in a lime-green tank top and cutoff jeans that were more unraveled fringe than actual shorts.

"Denise," Jillian said warningly, "this is Zachary Keller."

He took his hands off the sculpture self-consciously, dusted the right one on the seat of his pants and offered it to her. She just grinned and put her hands to her ample hips. "Establishment type, but at least he's very good-looking."

He felt nothing but warmth, friendliness and some rather intense weirdness emanating from her, and since handshakes were obviously too "establishment" to be acceptable, he pointed a finger at her and said, "Flower child born two decades too late, but at least she's very, *very* interesting."

Denise laughed and threw out her arms. "So what do you think of our little studio?"

He scratched an ear, trying to find a diplomatic way to say it. Jillian said it for him. "Our messy little studio, you mean."

Zach disciplined a grin, saying, "I don't know how you manage it, either of you. How do you create art out of all this chaos?"

Jillian shrugged. "You know what they say, beggars can't be choosers."

"What she really means," Denise said, bracing her forearms in the doorway, "is that witch sister of hers won't let her work out of her spacious home because chiseling stone leaves a little dust."

"A-actually, it leaves a lot of dust," Jillian said, quick to defend her sister, as always. "That's why I rigged up this." She moved to the end of the table beneath which the fan-in-a-box arrangement stood.

"I was wondering about that," he said. "Isn't the fan in backward?"

"Which is what makes it suck in the dust," she explained.

"Ah." He moved back there and went down on his haunches beside her, peeking into the box. He saw a series of screens and beneath them, in the very bottom, a pile of dust several inches deep. "Very clever."

"A clever, talented throw rug," said Denise. "That's our Jilly."

Jillian pushed up to her full height, and Zach followed suit. "Cut it out, Denise."

"Sorry, sugar, but you know perfectly well that you could set up shop in your sister's house without causing the Great Talking Head a moment's inconvenience, but you're going to continue to let her walk all over you."

"Are you saying I'm not welcome here anymore?" Jillian asked quietly.

"Don't get cute," Denise drawled.

"Then why the lecture?"

"I'm hoping that the fine bod here will have a tad more influence over you than I do, that's why. Besides, if you had your own place I wouldn't have to tell you that you can't work here today. Worly's got a gig, and the band has to practice."

"Think my power tools will throw a kink in things, huh?" Jillian said, grinning.

"Not the way they play," Denise cracked. Then she made a face. "Listen, kid, I'm sorry, but this is important."

"I understand," Jillian said. She picked up the cloth and she once more covered the work in progress, then looked at Zach. "Sorry you drove me all the way over here for nothing."

"It wasn't for nothing," he protested. "I got to see some of your work."

She smiled at that. "Well, I'll just hang out here for a while and then catch a bus home."

"I'll drive you," he told her, no longer surprised by what kept coming out of his mouth.

She shook her head. "No, that's all right."

Denise yawned loudly. "You two work it out," she said, turning away. "I'm going back to bed."

Jillian seemed a little shocked by the abandonment. Zach fastened a hand around her upper arm and turned her toward the door, saying, "I'll walk you out, at least."

Nodding, she let him steer her through the cluttered, dusty apartment and out onto the landing. She went down the stairs and out the door ahead of him, then stood on the sidewalk, staring at the bus stop on the corner, while he unlocked the car and went back for her.

"Get in."

She turned a considering stare on him. "Are you going after Eibersen today?"

"I'm going to try to track him down."

"I want to go with you."

Her statement caught him by surprise. He reeled mentally for an instant, then opened his mouth to refuse her.

"I can help," she stated hopefully. "If I go back to the house I'll just feel obligated to start washing walls. I'd rather help this way."

"No one can make you wash walls," he pointed out.

"That's not really the issue. I know Janzen. I can help, I'm sure of it."

He had to admit that she had a point. Still, it went against policy. "I don't know."

"Please. I need to help."

She did have a certain stake in this matter. Her sister was the target, after all. If the only reason he had for not letting her come along was personal... He pushed away the thought, not quite ready to think about that yet. So where did that leave him? Pushing up his sunglasses, he pinched the bridge of his nose.

"This kind of thing is really pretty dull work," he warned her.

"More dull than washing walls?" she retorted.

He couldn't argue that one. "I, um, have to go home and clean up first."

She knew capitulation when she heard it. Turning immediately, she moved toward the car, saying, "I don't mind."

This wasn't smart, and he knew it, but somehow he couldn't make himself care much at the moment. He watched her slide down into the passenger seat, then got in behind the wheel and started the car. It occurred to him as he drove around the block and headed downtown that nothing to do with this case was playing true to form, nothing and no one, but he couldn't quite put his finger on the reason for it. Then again, perhaps the reason for it was sitting next to him. She compelled him in a way he hadn't counted on, and that had upset his equilibrium. No doubt about it. And somehow, he had to get it back. But not now. Not just now.

She was impressed, and she told him so as they walked away from the valet who would park his sport car.

"Don't be," he said, escorting her across the marble-tiled foyer. "The building has some spectacular units, but mine isn't one of them, and even my little cubbyhole requires some heavy trade-off."

"In other words, you're not as successful as you seem?" she asked, knowing full well that he did a good deal of pro bono work.

"I do all right," he said, "but I had help getting started."

"That's nothing to be ashamed of."

"I didn't say it was."

They walked toward a uniformed security guard at a small desk, behind which stood two banks of three elevators each, facing each other. "Eugene, this is Jillian Waltham."

Eugene stood and doffed his hat. "Miss."

She noticed that as soon as they'd passed him, he flipped open a book and wrote down something in it. "Does he always do that?" she whispered, nodding in his direction as they waited for the elevator. The doors slid open on the left before Zach could reply.

"Only when I give him a name," he said, ushering her on board and pushing the button numbered four. "Once you're in the book," he explained, "you can go up without waiting for permission. Otherwise, you have to stand down here while he calls upstairs to ask if you're allowed."

She smiled at that. So he'd purposefully put her "in the book," had he? She tried not to assign too much importance to it, but she couldn't help wondering if he brought many women here with him and just how many of their names he gave to the guard.

The elevator delivered them quickly and smoothly to the fourth floor, where they disembarked midway along a wide, well-lit corridor. Again, they turned to the left. Six doors down on the right, he stopped and took out two sets of keys. After fitting one key from one ring into the top lock and another into the lower, he turned both, then opened the door a crack, extracted both keys, pocketed them and pushed the door wide. "Make yourself at home," he said, going in first to flip on lights.

It really wasn't very big. A dark central hall led to a small living area with a narrow balcony overlooking Turtle Creek. It was furnished with a single chair upholstered in black leather, a television set and several pieces of workout equipment. Opposite the balcony was a bar counter; shutters above it closed off the kitchen. One end wall was ceiling-to-floor shelves, the contents of which she wanted to study further. The kitchen and bedroom opened off the hallway at the front of the apartment. He allowed her to stick her head in both rooms, saying, "Nothing much to see, I'm afraid."

The kitchen was small and done in black and white, with recessed lights above the high-gloss black cabinets. He had shoved an old desk into one corner and obviously used it for a makeshift home office. A small, top-line notebook computer sat open on the battered desk next to a canister of beef jerky. The counters were bare, the sink empty except for a single drinking glass. The bedroom was tiny and dark, furnished cheaply with a mismatched queen-sized bed, dresser and bedside table. A brass lamp on a

swing arm had been mounted on the wall at the head of the bed.
The bed was unmade; the dresser mirror was hung with clothing:
a shirt, a pair of jeans, a tie and belt. A newspaper lay folded on
the floor beside the bed. Curiously, an alarm clock and book sat
on the floor beneath the bedside table, which was bare on top.
An open door revealed a small bathroom with one towel on the
floor and another draped over the edge of the sink.

"Seen enough?"

She drew back into the hallway, blushing. "Sorry. I didn't
mean to pry."

He grinned. "I didn't think you were. I figure it's a female
thing. My mother always checks to be sure I'm not leaving my
socks and underwear on the floor."

Jillian laughed. "She'd be proud, then. No socks, no underwear."

"That's because I sent the laundry out yesterday," he admitted
shamelessly.

She followed him back into the living room. He went to the
shelving unit and picked up a remote control, which he put into
her hand.

"TV, radio, CD player. Amuse yourself. I'll be quick."

"No problem."

He went off to clean up. Within seconds she heard the sound
of water running. She studied the remote, aimed it and turned on
the radio. Then she began cataloging the contents of his shelves.

The photos drew her eye first: a middle-aged couple in jeans
and hats standing arm-in-arm in front of a corral; a young Zach
in a police officer's uniform flanked by two other men who bore
him a strong resemblance and, therefore, must be his brothers; a
formal portrait of three small children that bore the handwritten
message "We love you, Uncle Zach." She smiled and turned
her attention to the spines of a row of hardback books. He liked
techno thrillers, military biographies and westerns. In addition,
he kept a number of law books and college texts dealing with
criminal justice studies. A stack of magazines revealed the male
standards: sports, cars, computers. She found a chart detailing
dietary requirements and the uses of herbal and vitamin supple-

ments. All these things were interesting and revealing, but they were not the items that most intrigued her. What truly interested her were the "decorative" items scattered among the rest: an eggshell ceramic bowl, a brick inscribed with what looked like runes, a ranch scene in silhouette cut from a pair of Mexican spurs and, most interesting of all, a small stone sculpture that was part horse and part '57 Chevy. She lifted it and looked at the bottom, her eyebrows rising when she saw the name of the artist inscribed there.

"It was a gift," he said, startling her.

She whirled to find him standing in the doorway. Her eyeballs nearly popped. He looked good enough to eat, in boots, crisply creased jeans, western belt and a pale-yellow, torso-hugging T-shirt that delineated every cut and swell of a chest that had been sculpted in this very room. His cleanly shaved face seemed chiseled of bronze stone, and his dark hair curled damply against his forehead. He extracted a comb from his back pocket and swept his hair back as he walked toward her. Jillian made herself turn calmly and replace the sculpture on the shelf.

"The giver has excellent taste," she said.

"Had," he told her, coming to her side. He slid the comb into his back pocket and gestured toward the shelves before folding his arms. "I don't know about taste, frankly, but Serena had a knack for knowing exactly what I would like. These were all gifts from her, and they aren't all she gave me. I told you I'd had help getting started. She left me sixty thousand dollars in her will."

"And you put it to good work rescuing victims of stalkers and domestic abuse," Jillian said, smiling. "Your secretary brags."

"I've noticed that." He stared down at her, smiling. "I didn't realize the two of you were such good friends, though."

She shrugged. "Lois is easy to talk to."

He burst out with a laugh. "No, you're easy to talk to. With Lois, about all you can do is listen."

She smiled. "Maybe so."

He narrowed his eyes as if trying to figure something out. "You remind me of her, you know."

She knew that he wasn't comparing her with his garrulous secretary. "You mentioned that before."

"It's not looks so much," he said, almost to himself. "You're built similarly, but the rest is completely different. It's more...I don't know, personality, I guess." Her eyebrows shot upward at that, and he smiled. "Serena was a sweet, generous woman with a quirky sense of humor and a very personal sense of style. Even after she made it big modeling, she never thought she was anything special, and that made her very easy to be with. Her appreciation for what she considered her good luck made her a lot of fun."

Jillian swallowed, torn between hopeful flattery and sheer envy. "You must have loved each other very much," she said softly.

"We were crazy about each other," he said, "and I miss her, but we were a long way from settling down."

"Still, she was very important to you."

He nodded. "She had a profound impact on my life. What happened to her shouldn't have happened to anyone, but especially not to her, and I owe it to her to keep it from happening again."

"You must know that you're not to blame for what happened to her."

"I understand that others are more to blame," he said.

She smiled up into his soft green eyes. Perhaps he still felt some guilt over what had happened to Serena, but she could see that he had dealt with his loss and made something good come of it. She admired that, very much, and she meant to tell him so, but when she opened her mouth what came out was, "I'm glad you're free now."

He blinked and jerked slightly, as if she'd taken an unexpected swing at him. Color flooded her cheeks; the heat of embarrassment rose in her throat and threatened to choke her.

"I—I shouldn't have said that! I didn't mean—"

"Are you saying you're attracted to me?"

She could have laughed. "Do you really have to ask?"

"How would I know otherwise?"

"How could you not? Every woman who knows you is attracted to you."

His grin turned her heart over. "Is that so?"

"All the girls in the deli have huge crushes on you."

His green eyes drilled her. "What about you?"

She gulped, thinking, Especially me, but she said, as nonchalantly as possible, "I certainly understand why they feel that way."

"Do you?" His gaze dropped to her mouth.

She knew that she could turn away and derail what was going to happen next, but she stood her ground, amazed at herself, and said, "Yes."

He reached out a hand to clamp it around the back of her neck. "I shouldn't be doing this," he said, even as he pulled her to him.

Her brain went on autopilot. She heard herself saying inanely, "No?"

"No." He widened his stance and snaked his free arm around her waist, curling it tight and bringing her closer still. "Definitely not," he said, even as his mouth covered hers.

She closed her eyes, her hands clasping the tops of his shoulders. His lips moved against hers, sliding and nipping. When he licked the corner of her mouth with the tip of his tongue, she opened for him. Groaning, he fit his mouth over hers and plunged deep. Liquid heat speared through her. In response she wrapped her arms around his neck, leaned into him and slid her tongue against his. Suddenly she was being devoured with lips, tongue, teeth and hands. Her feet edged forward, so that she was standing essentially between his legs, her body welded to his from pelvis to chest. She could not mistake the fact that he wanted more—and that she wanted to give it to him. Long moments later, he began to pull back in increments. When at last his mouth left hers and she managed to lever open her eyes, it was to find him looking down at her with an intently troubled expression on his face.

"I really shouldn't have done that," he said, dropping his hands and stepping back. "I mean, I *really* shouldn't have done that.'' He rubbed the heels of his hands across his temples, slicking down the sides of his damp hair. "I really do have a policy against this kind of thing. It's dangerous to get emotionally involved with clients."

"I understand," she said, nodding.

"It complicates everything, skews my judgment. It...it's just not smart."

She took a deep breath, trying to calm the excitement rioting through her body. "You're right. Of course you're right."

He bowed his head, looking up at her from beneath the jut of his brow. A smile crept across his face. She felt her own breaking out in response.

He shook his head as if wondering which of them was the biggest fool. "We have work to do," he said.

She cleared her throat. "We should go."

He lifted his hand, palm out, and suddenly she knew exactly what she was doing, exactly what she wanted. With startling clarity, she understood that she'd already jeopardized this. It hadn't really happened yet, and already she was in danger of blowing it. She should have told him everything from the beginning, no matter what Camille said or did, but she hadn't, and now she was stuck. If she told him now, this kiss might as well have never happened. If she told him later, at least she might have something to lose, not that it was ever going to be dreams coming true with him. Wanting to kiss her was a long way from being in love with her. He'd said himself that he'd been wild about Serena and nowhere near ready to settle down with her. She couldn't expect even that much from him, really. But she could feel the magic for a while. She lifted her hand and placed it in his, as silent as the grave.

Chapter Five

They rode the elevator down to the lobby, then let themselves out into the parking garage. He made himself let go of her hand as they approached his parking niche.

"We'll take the workhorse," Zach said, indicating the battered ten-year-old, three-quarter-ton pickup occupying the space next to his beloved convertible. "It's less conspicuous, and I don't mind banging it up, if I have to."

"What do you mean, banging it up?" she asked as he handed her up into the passenger side.

It was already sweltering in the garage, and he knew the inside of the truck was like an oven, so he hurried around and got in to start the engine and the air conditioner. "Sometimes," he explained, letting the engine idle a minute or so, "I get made. The bad guy recognizes me, and he usually doesn't like being tailed and watched. I've had them attack my vehicle with everything from their fists to a riding lawn mower. Sometimes they think they have to run away, and they actually bash into me, but not in this baby. There's something about heavy-duty chrome bumpers and grill protectors that makes even maniacs think twice."

"I see why you don't want to take the convertible," she said, appearing not in the least bothered by the prospect of getting rammed.

"Think Eibersen is violent enough to bash my truck?"

She shook her head. "No. I can't say he wouldn't do something stupid if pushed far enough, though."

"He's already done something stupid," Zach pointed out.

"I mean, something intentionally violent, at least toward Camille."

"But you don't think he'll take me on?"

"Not on his best day."

He nodded and put the five-speed transmission in gear. "I'll keep that in mind." He started the vehicle moving and reached for the radio knob, only to find that she had reached for it, too. Grinning, he sat back and let her take care of the music while he concentrated on his driving.

They must have made ten stops that morning, checking known hangouts and friends of Eibersen's, asking questions, waiting and watching. Early on, conversation featured the basic premise and standard operating procedures for tracking and tailing someone, as well as the kind of interventions he could legally perform. Jillian was enthralled, but during lunch at a coffee shop on the far east side of Mesquite, the topic of conversation changed to Jillian and her art.

"When did you know you wanted to be an artist?" he asked.

No one had ever asked her that before, and Jillian had to think about it. "I can't recall a time when I wanted to be anything else, actually—except the standard stuff."

"Standard stuff?" he echoed, picking up his hamburger to take a huge bite out of it.

She nodded, scraping sesame seeds off her bun with a fingertip. "You know, wife and mom. Other than that, an artist is all I ever wanted to be."

He wiped his mouth, and she noticed that he didn't look up from his plate to make eye contact with her. "How did you meet your friend Denise and her musician husband?"

She accepted the change in subject with a tinge of disappointment. "We all met in college at North Texas."

"UNT, that's Denton, right?"

Jillian nodded. "It's a good art school, but it's a top-notch music school."

"How come you wound up there?"

She shrugged. "It was the best school within driving distance that I could afford."

"You had a car then, huh?"

"I still have a car."

He laid down the hamburger and wiped his fingers on a paper napkin as thin as cheap tissue. This time the gaze that he lifted to hers was as sharp as broken glass. "That was your car you let Gerry commandeer this morning?"

"Hers was in the shop."

He shook his head, and she recognized the flash of anger that brightened his eyes. "Holy cow, Jillian, don't you ever stand up for yourself?"

She took a deep breath and toyed with a potato chip on the edge of her plate. "Zach, you have to understand that Gerry—"

"Took you in after your father had dumped her for your mother. Yeah, I know, but, honey, you can't let them walk all over you the way they do! You need—"

She leaned forward and laid a hand on his wrist, cutting off the flow of his words.

"What I don't need is to hurt anyone," she said gently.

"You wouldn't hurt a fly!" he scoffed.

"Just my existence hurts Gerry," she said. "I feel sorry for her, Zach. Can you understand that? She's a damaged human being."

He stared at her a moment longer, then shook his head. "I don't know how you can be so understanding, when she treats you like some kind of lower life form."

"We have more in common that you realize," she told him. "We both loved my father, and Camille is all either of us have now that he's gone."

Something very like pity flashed across his face, only to be replaced in a blink by a mask of unconcern. "It won't always be that way," he said almost dismissively, attacking his hamburger again.

"You're right," she said, hoping that it was so.

He polished off his burger and watched impatiently as she nibbled on hers. Finally, she cut off the part she'd munched on with her fork and offered the rest to him. He gulped it down in two bites, and they were off again, chasing after one lead and another.

About midafternoon, as she was sitting in the idling truck fighting boredom and trying to keep cool while Zach purchased soft drinks in a convenience store, an old British import pulled up into the space next to her. Something about it triggered her interest, and she turned her head just as the driver got out. She nearly fell out of her seat when she recognized Janzen Eibersen. His straight blond hair had grown longer, almost to the tip of his chin, and was worn brushed back from the brow without a part and hanging about his lean face. Reflexively, she ducked down, but he paid her no mind, hurrying toward the store while digging into his hip pocket. His lanky frame bore an oversized tank top, baggy safari shorts and dirty high-top tennis shoes so old and worn that they looked as if they could be pulled apart by hand. A few days' growth of blond beard shadowed his lower face, individual hairs glistening in the strong sunlight. All in all, he looked about as different from the slavishly well-groomed fashion plate who had escorted her sister about town as it was possible to do so.

Jillian felt her heart pounding. What if some sixth sense alerted him that he was being watched? What if he saw and recognized her? Her heart climbed up into her throat. Only God knew what he would say or do.

Just as he reached the front of the store, the door swung open and Zach came through it carrying two large soft drink cups and a small brown paper bag. He didn't blink so much as an eyelash in recognition of his quarry as he walked past him. Jillian bit down ruthlessly on the urge to scream out an identification. Janzen breezed into the store without a pause. Jillian reached over and opened the truck door for Zach. Hugging the drinks to his chest, he tossed the paper bag onto the seat.

"Zach, that was—"

"Stay cool, sweetheart. We don't want him to know we recognized him."

"But he's—"

"Take the drink, Jillian, and sit still."

She took the drink. Zach wedged his between his thighs and reached for the ignition. The old truck rumbled to life, and Zach threw it into Reverse. Contrary to expectations, however, he didn't act particularly excited. Instead, he calmly backed the truck around and headed it down the street.

"Did Eibersen spot you?" he asked as they drove away.

"I don't think so."

"You're certain?"

"I don't think he even looked at me."

"Okay. Maybe this is our lucky day, then."

"What are we going to do?" Even as she asked it, he put on the turn blinker and slowed the truck.

"We're going to wait and follow him when he leaves that store lot," Zach said, pulling over in front of a used-car dealership.

"What if he turns in the other direction?"

"No problem." He pointed to a small door in her side of the dash. "Look in the glove compartment and hand me those binoculars."

She opened the compartment and picked the binoculars out of a jumble of maps, flashlights and a heavy truncheon. The binoculars were surprisingly lightweight. A peck on her window made her jerk in that direction. A man with dark, oily hair displayed his gold caps for her.

"Roll down your window," Zach said. She rolled it down.

"You folks interested in trading this old heap?" the man asked brightly.

Zach took the binoculars out of Jillian's hands, smiling at the man. "Nope, not today. We're just trying to read the street numbers on some of these buildings. Hey, you interested in getting your number painted on the curb?"

The man waved a hand in disappointed rejection and walked away. Jillian stared at Zach. What on earth was he up to? He was up to craning his neck around and targeting the binoculars on the slender space between a tree and a metal storage building at the edge of the car lot. "What was that numbers stuff all about?" she asked.

He answered without looking at her. "Explains the binoculars and gets him out of our hair. Nothing sends a salesman in the other direction as fast as somebody else trying to sell him something."

"Clever," she muttered.

"Here comes our boy," he said at the same time, dropping the binoculars on the seat. He put the transmission into gear, but then he calmly dug into the brown bag on the seat between them and extracted a package of peanuts. "Want some?" he asked, tearing open the cellophane. "There's another package."

"Peanuts?"

"You didn't eat much lunch," he said, glancing over his shoulder. "Peanuts are high protein," he went on, watching Janzen drive right by them.

"Aren't we going after him?" Jillian asked, thoroughly puzzled.

Zach popped a handful of peanuts into his mouth. "You bet." He chewed, letting several more cars drive by. He wiped his hand on his jeans and finally pulled out, saying, "Pick up those binoculars and get a bead on him, will you?"

Exasperated, she snatched up the binoculars and trained them on the traffic ahead. Surprisingly, she had a pretty good vantage point, sitting high in that old truck. It occurred to her that Janzen would never know he was being watched. Clever was an understatement when it came to Zach Keller. She watched while Zach drove and munched.

"He's turning left at the next light," she announced. To her surprise, Zach suddenly sped up, weaving in and out of traffic and just making the turn before the signal changed. He immediately backed off again.

"See him?" he asked.

It took a second or two to get reoriented through the binoculars, but then she spotted the British-made car. "Got him."

"Good work. We'll just hang back so we don't get made and see where he leads us."

She grinned at the compliment. Looked like they were making a pretty good team. A thought occurred. "How do you do this when you're alone?"

"One hand for the wheel, one hand for the binoculars," he replied complacently. She lowered the binoculars to give him a disapproving look, and he laughed. "Either that or I have to drive a lot closer to the target."

She turned back to the binoculars. "He's signaling left again, but he has to turn through traffic this time."

Zach switched lanes as she spoke, slowing so that he came up two cars behind Janzen. When Janzen turned into the drive-through lane of a dry cleaner, Zach drove on past, changing lanes and pulling into a parking space about a block away on the opposite side of the street.

"Put down the binoculars," he said.

And she realized that she was holding them at chest height, clearly visible through the window. He shifted slightly, aiming his gaze out her window, and nonchalantly spread his arm along the back of the seat.

"So, ready to take up sleuthing for a living?" he asked conversationally.

She wrinkled her nose. "I think I'd rather grind away at my rocks, thank you."

He chuckled. "Told you it was boring."

"Depends on the company," she said blithely.

His gaze focused on her face. "So it does." Then he was staring out the window once more. Suddenly he shifted in his seat. "Here we go again."

She was not surprised when he waited patiently for Janzen to drive past them this time, and she didn't need to be told when to take up the binoculars.

After almost an hour, they finally trailed Janzen to an old motel that rented units by the week and month. He had parked the car and was unloading the clothing, beer and groceries he had picked up along the way.

"Bingo," Zach said as they drove past. He pulled over down the street and made some notes in his notebook, then shoved the binoculars back into the glove compartment and pulled out his cell phone. He made two calls, informing whoever was on the other end of Janzen's whereabouts and ordering twenty-four-hour surveillance. "Don't worry," he said into the phone, winking at Jillian. "The client can afford it." He put away the phone and drove on. "Okay, we've run him to the ground. I've got an operative on the way now. Next time he steps wrong, we'll have him dead to rights."

"What happens then?"

"Your sister presses charges, and our problems are solved."

Jillian tried to sigh with relief, but two things bothered her suddenly. For one thing, it just seemed too easy. For another, when it was over, she'd have no more excuse to see Zach Keller. She voiced neither concern, however, and instead tried to take comfort in the idea that Janzen Eibersen might finally be on his way out of their lives for good.

She had been a champ. He hadn't heard a word of complaint all day, and he'd known darn few partners with such amiability. Moreover, she was sweet and gentle and understanding—too understanding, if you asked him, at least when it came to her sister and her sister's mother. Not that it was any of his business. He ought to keep out of it. He intended to keep out of it, but she provoked a protective instinct in him that he'd never known before, not even with Serena. In truth, if he'd been a little more protective of Serena, she might still be alive. This protectiveness with Jillian troubled him, though. She wasn't his client, and she wasn't his girlfriend, even if he had let compulsion override his good sense when he'd kissed her. Yet he couldn't shake the feeling that he should be concentrating on protecting her. He shook his head, puzzled by his own behavior and emotions. She noticed.

"What's wrong?"

"Wrong?" He smiled. "Nothing. Why?"

"I don't know, you seemed troubled."

He dredged up a believable lie. "I was just thinking about how, after all our hard work, we lucked onto Eibersen in the end."

She thought about that, her hand languidly ruffling her wispy hair. "It wasn't all luck," she said. "We were in the right neighborhood because the trail took us there."

"True, but sometimes I hang out in the right neighborhood for days before I latch onto someone."

"Then I guess we were lucky," she said with a shrug. He smiled and tried not to notice the long, creamy length of her slender legs when she crossed them. She folded her hands in her lap and said, "I thought we made a pretty good team today, though."

Something leaped inside him, something gleeful and hopeful, something wary and dismayed. He didn't trust himself to speak, so he merely nodded and tried to concentrate on his driving. A flutter of sensation at the back of his neck prompted him to lift a hand and rub the spot. He'd been on edge all day in some way that he couldn't quite put his finger on, and it didn't have a darn thing to do with Eibersen or anyone else but the lady sitting next to him. With that silent admission, the flutter of sensation dropped to his groin. He sat up straight, irritated with himself. She laid her head against the window and hummed along with the music from the radio. The sound crawled over him inch by antsy inch like a physical touch. Did she know how sexy that husky voice was? He couldn't believe that she did.

It was with profound relief that he turned down the street where she lived. She sat up straight and nervously fluffed her hair with both hands. He guided the truck to the curb and to a stop. His arm went out, bridging the backs of their seats. "Thanks for your help today."

She smiled. "Thanks for taking me along."

His hand reached, of its own volition, to tweak a strand of hair that curved against her cheek. The realization that he wanted to kiss her again hit him with all the weight of a sledgehammer. He took his hand back, very slowly and deliberately, hoping she wouldn't notice. The way she glanced down at her lap seemed to indicate that she did. She reached for the door handle, and he heard himself saying, "Don't forget to punch in the deactivation code after you open the door."

"I won't."

"You do remember the code, don't you?"

Jillian laughed. The sound moved up her throat in slow, husky ripples that threatened to mesmerize him. "I'm hardly likely to forget," she said, or it was something very like it. His mouth was dry, a condition he'd been fighting all day.

He tried to swallow, made himself smile and said, "Have a good evening."

"You, too," she said, letting herself out of the truck and climbing down to the ground. She closed the door, gave him a little wave through the window and moved off up the walk.

His gaze went to her rear end like a magnet to a lodestone. She didn't walk like fashion models, legs crossing in front of each another, hips swaying exaggeratedly. Instead, she walked like a kid, all but skipping with a kind of elemental innocence that both shocked and drew him. He remembered the way she'd kissed him back, the tensile strength in her slender arms, the thrust of her breasts against his chest, the way her mouth parted beneath his, her tongue curling and tangling. A shiver ran through him. She was no kid. She was a woman, all woman, and his body had recognized her as such even before his muddled mind had. He'd do best to keep his distance from now on.

She opened the door, disappeared for an instant, then returned to wave a farewell. He didn't even realize he was waiting for that wave until it came. He answered it with one of his own, then pulled the truck away from the curb, his attention resolutely trained out the windshield. Distance. Yes, from now on he'd definitely keep his distance.

He drove home, aware of the heat in a way he hadn't been before. Why was it that everything seemed to have changed? The radio music suddenly irritated him, so he turned it off. The sun literally radiated through his untinted windshield, magnifying and sizzling. He turned the air conditioner up to its highest setting and tried to plan his evening. A cold plate of *arroz con pollo*, chicken in rice Mexican-style, that waited in his refrigerator would make a fine dinner. He'd watch the early news, write a brief report on the day's activities, work out, shower, read a little and turn in early. He was expected to spend the day with his family tomorrow, starting with church. He wondered if Jillian would be attending church somewhere tomorrow morning and immediately turned off the thought.

After parking the truck himself in its usual spot, he went up to the apartment and changed his clothes. Donning knit shorts and athletic shoes, he put the *arroz con pollo* in the microwave. When it was steaming, he topped it with salsa and sour cream and wolfed it down with corn chips and rolled tortillas. The peppers singed his mouth, but he hardly tasted them somehow. After rinsing and swabbing the plate and fork he'd used, he stacked them in the drainer and moved into the living room to switch on the television and listen to the news. He deliberately turned on Camille's station, but she was not a weekend anchor, and he soon lost interest. Apparently nothing noteworthy had happened anywhere that day, because he couldn't seem to concentrate on the national news, either. Switching off the television set, he went back to the kitchen and sat down at the desk.

He typed out a brief report on his laptop computer, saved it and glanced at his wristwatch. It was appallingly early yet. He toyed with the notion of calling up one of his buddies and suggesting some activity, bowling, maybe, or billiards, but when he tried to think of whom to call, he couldn't think of anyone with whom he really wanted to spend time. Restlessly, he moved back into the living room and took up position among his workout equipment.

As usual, he lost himself in the physical exertion and mindless repetitions, working himself into a pleasant state of exhaustion. Sweaty and satisfied, he walked into the bedroom, stripped and went into the bathroom to turn on the shower. He let the hot water massage his muscles, shampooed his hair and scrubbed his body. The tiny room was filled with fog by the time he stepped out of the shower and reached for his towel. He felt relaxed and in control. After drying off, he wrapped a fresh towel around his hips and went into the bedroom. Folding back the covers, he swept out the bed with his hand, then sat down on the edge of it and reached for the book on the floor beneath his bedside table. That was when he saw the clock.

It was just past eight, far too early to call it a night. What was Jillian doing? Scrubbing walls? He mentally jerked back from such thoughts and snatched up the book. Reclining, he opened it to the marker and began to read. Hours later, he yawned and bent down to look at the clock on the floor beside the bed. Thirty-five minutes. He'd been reading thirty-five lousy minutes and couldn't remember a single word of what he'd read. God help him.

Determined to turn off his mind and sleep, he hit the lamp, shoved away the towel and pulled up the covers. Sometime later, he drifted off to sleep. The ringing of his cell phone in the deep dark of night disturbed an embarrassingly erotic dream. Rubbing his face with one hand, he grabbed for the phone with the other. Only when his rough greeting was answered by the familiar voice of a man did Zach fully realize that he had expected to hear Jillian on the other end. It took a moment to put a name to the voice.

"Gabler?"

"Yeah. Listen, I hate to say it, but I lost him. Sorry."

Zach's mind whirled into full cognizance. He sat up, hissing a particular curse. "What happened? Did Eibersen know you were on him?"

"Looks that way. I can't figure how he spotted me, though. It was almost as if he had the slip set up before he left the room."

Zach went cold. That meant he could have screwed up himself. Eibersen had either spotted his truck on the tail or he had recognized Jillian and stayed so cool about it that she hadn't realized she'd been made. Neither boded well for his client this night, however. He shot up from the bed and carried the phone into the closet, swatting at the switch on the wall that controlled the overhead light. "How far are you from the Waltham house?"

"I'm still in Mesquite."

"Damn." He squinted in the brightness, yanking at jeans and such.

"Padgett's closer. I'll give him a ring and tell him to meet you there."

"Right," Zach said, shimmying into clothes. "Then you get back to Eibersen's room and see if he's blown the joint."

"Will do."

Zach clipped the phone to his belt and stomped into his boots, remembering what had happened the last time Eibersen had decided to pay a visit to his former fiancée. He hoped this controlled panic was for nothing. The security system was activated, after all. If Eibersen was at Camille's, the cops would be on their way, too. Still, Zach couldn't help feeling that something wasn't right and that he, ultimately, was responsible. Grabbing his keys and wallet, he literally ran out of the building.

He decided on the truck and was soon squealing his tires as he took the curves down the garage ramp to the street. He tried to tell himself to slow down, calm down, but a strange panic was building in him, a certainty of wrongness and threat. He ran a red light at a deserted intersection, praying no enforcement cameras had been mounted at that site, and sped on. Within minutes he was pulling up in front of Camille's house.

Killing the engine, he sat in the darkened silence, waiting for his senses to tell him that everything was all right, but the sense of wrongness built. He grabbed the binoculars from the glove compartment and checked the surrounding landscape. He saw a battered, once-silver English-built car at the end of the block behind some bushes. The binoculars fell to the floor as he bounded out of the truck and ran to the house. At the front door, he paused again, trying to order his thoughts. No alarm was wailing. If Eibersen was trying to get inside, it would sound. The best thing he, Zach, could do right now was scout the perimeter. He started to turn away, but a glance in the long, narrow window flanking the front door momentarily froze him in place.

The keypad for the security system was mounted on the wall right behind the door, and as he watched, one number after another silently lit. Seven. One. Seven. Damn! Someone was key-ing in the deactivation code on the other pad. Galvanized, Zach punched the doorbell over and over while pounding on the door and screaming for Jillian at the top of his lungs. Then he took off at a dead run around the end of the house toward the back door. He skidded around the corner, and a figure all in black whizzed past him. Fighting the impulse to check Jillian first, he turned and went after the perpetrator, but it was too late; whoever it was—and he had no doubt that it was Eibersen but no proof, either—had melted into the night. Doggedly, he ran toward the spot where he'd seen the car parked, but long before he got there, the car rolled away silently, its lights off. Zach cursed loud and long. If only he'd brought the binoculars he might have been able to get a license plate number, something to tie that car to Janzen Eibersen and Eibersen to a possible break-in.

Defeated, Zach jogged back to the house. He went to the front door and rang the bell until Camille came to let him in.

"What on earth? Was that you a few minutes ago?"

He brushed past her, demanding more gruffly than he'd in-tended, "Where's Jillian?"

"In bed, I assume. What the devil is this about?"

"Eibersen was here," he told her, striding through the house. "Here? But—"

He left her standing in the den as he strode through the house. The back door was standing open, just as he'd known it would be. Catching up with him, Camille gasped. "What'd you ex-pect?" Zach snapped. "If you'd had the locks changed like I told you to..."

"But the security sys—"

She suddenly clamped her mouth shut, and he had a pretty good idea why. Rage surged through him, and he countered it by walking away from her. He needed to see Jillian, to be sure she was okay. A door opened into the hallway, revealing Gerry standing in a rectangle of light.

"What is it?"

"Ask your daughter," he snapped, moving on to Jillian's door. Raising his hand to knock, he aborted the effort and grasped the doorknob, instead. Fragmented light from the open doorway showed him a sleeping form huddled in the center of a full-sized bed. Only then did his heartbeat slow to something near normal. Quietly, Zach walked across the floor and looked down at the bed. She lay on her side, one hand tucked beneath her cheek. Even in this dim light he could trace the pattern of a blue vein that lined one eyelid.

"Jillian?"

She jerked slightly, then her eyelids fluttered and lifted as she rolled to her back. "Zach?" She smiled lazily; then her eyes went wide in panic. "What's wrong?"

He sat down just as she jerked upright, and suddenly she was in his arms, her heart beating wildly. "It's all right, honey. I got here in time to scare him off."

"Janzen?" She pulled back just enough to push her hair out of her eyes and exhale her relief. Puzzlement rushed in behind it. "But your men—"

Zach winced. "He gave us the slip somehow, which means that he knew we were watching him. Jillian, are you absolutely sure he didn't recognize you today?"

She bit her lip. "If he did, he gave absolutely no sign of it."

Zach sighed. "Whether he made us or the sub, he's still smarter than I gave him credit for. But that doesn't explain how he knew the deactivation code to the security system."

Jillian moaned. Someone coughed behind him, and he released Jillian to turn in that direction. Camille and Gerry crowded the doorway. Camille was staring at Jillian. Gerry was studying her toenails. Zach realized for the first time that Gerry's uncovered hair was steel-gray, about an inch long and plastered to her skull like paint. He also realized that he'd been left out in the dark about something important. Getting up off the bed, he brought his hands to his hips and took a deliberate measure of each of the three women. None of them would look at him. He struggled to tamp down his temper.

"All right, who gave out the code? And who did you give it to?"

No one said a word. He bit back the explosion waiting to erupt and took a deep breath.

"He knew the code. I saw the numbers lighting up on the key pad. You get two tries with this system before it alarms. He couldn't have pulled those numbers out of the air. Somebody had to—"

"He could have guessed," Jillian said in a small voice.

"Five digits," Zach pointed out, targeting her. "I watched the first three punched in correctly. He obviously got the other two, because I'm not hearing any alarm, am I? What are the odds of guessing five correct digits on the second try? He knew that number, damn it!"

Jillian swallowed. "What I mean is, he could have guessed that the code was one of our birth dates."

Birth date. No. Surely not. No one could be that stupid, but when he whipped a stare in Camille's direction, he saw confirmation in the bowed head and the grim line of her mouth. He had to swallow twice before he could get the next question out.

"Who...whose birth date?"

"Mine," Jillian said softly.

He closed his eyes and balled his hands into fists in an effort to hold at bay the anger crowding him. "Did no one," he asked in a low voice shaking with suppressed fury, "consider that a former fiancé just might remember *family birth dates?*" He roared at the end; he couldn't help it. "What in heaven's name were you thinking?" he demanded of Camille.

"You pressured me!" she wailed. "I couldn't think of anything else!"

"So you used your sister's birth date! And it never occurred to you that he might know it, might remember it! How stupid is that? Why didn't you just use your own? He wouldn't have needed a second try then!"

"I didn't think it mattered!"

"Didn't matter?" he bawled. "Are you insane?"

"I thought *you* would take care of him!" she cried. "I thought you would have it under control by now! Excuse me for having so much faith in the great Zach Keller!"

He was trying to devise a suitable comeback to that and maintain his tenuous hold on his temper at the same time when she did the unexpected and burst into tears. He'd wager that he looked no more horrified than Gerry did, but the unexpected display of vulnerability did cool his anger somewhat. "There's no need for that," he grumbled. "We'll just change the code and—"

His phone rang, and he snatched it off his belt like a drowning man grasping a lifeline. "What?"

It was Padgett. As luck would have it, he'd picked up Eibersen on his way over to the Walthams' and trailed him back to the motel, where he showed every sign of staying put. Brief questioning revealed that Eibersen had exited his car dressed in shorts, T-shirt and sandals. The black garb worn during the break-in was not in evidence. No doubt he'd tossed it out the window or crammed it under the seat before Padgett came across him. Frustrated, Zach hung up and reported the conversation.

"So where does that leave us?" Jillian asked from his bed.

"Square one, that's where," Gerry said scathingly. "He's still out there, and we have no protection!"

"We'll change the code in the morning," Zach muttered.

"And what about tonight?" Gerry demanded.

"I have a man watching him."

"You had a man watching him earlier!" she snapped, and it didn't help that she was absolutely right. She folded her arms imperiously. "You'll just have to stay and guard us."

Camille sniffed dramatically. "I—I won't sleep a wink if you don't. I'm not even sure I can sleep in my own room if you don't check it out first."

Zach barely restrained the urge to roll his eyes. "I hardly think—"

Camille lifted her eyelids, fluttering them prettily as big drops rolled over their rims and down her cheeks. "It's wearing me down," she said weepily. "I'm so tired of it all."

Zach felt like the world's biggest heel, despite the fact that she was as responsible for this mess as he was, if not more so. He couldn't think what to do beyond stepping forward to awkwardly pat her shoulder. "You just need some sleep," he told her.

When she turned to him and pressed her face to his chest, he was taken aback. After a long, awkward moment of trying to decide what to do with his arms, he reluctantly looped them around her, casting a look at Jillian over his shoulder at the same time. The very blankness of her expression told him far more than he wanted to know. She couldn't hide the envy and uncertainty in her huge, expressive eyes. He felt disloyal somehow, and it irked him. She was nothing to him. He owed her nothing. At the same time, it irritated him that she could think he might come to like her sister better than her. He dropped his arms to his sides and stepped back from Camille, who sniffed and dabbed at her eyes with her fingertips.

"I won't sleep a wink if you don't stay," she said breathlessly.

Zach sighed inwardly and nodded acquiescence. He looked again at Jillian lying in her bed, one arm curled beneath her head, her slight form gently twisted beneath the covers. Images from his disturbed dreams flashed before his mind's eye, and he knew that he wasn't going to sleep any more this night anyway. She drew him, literally, so that he was walking toward her before he even realized what he was doing. He didn't know quite what to do with himself when he got there, but he knew that he couldn't stand there staring down at her without touching her. Carefully, he straightened the edge of her covers and brushed his fingertips across her forehead, fighting the urge to press his lips there, instead.

"Get some sleep," he said. "I'll hang around till morning."

She nodded and rolled onto her side. Thankfully, she would never know how hard it was for him to turn his back then and walk away.

Chapter Six

Zach closed the door to Jillian's room behind him. "Try to get some sleep," he told the pair flanking him. "If you're not up in the morning when I have to leave, I'll set the security system before I go."

"What about the code?" Gerry asked.

"I'll take care of that before I go and write the new code on a card that I'll slip under the bedroom door."

"Speaking of which," Camille said, sniffing, "I know it's foolish, but I'd really appreciate it if you'd check my room, just to be sure he didn't open any windows or anything like that."

Zach allowed himself the luxury of rolling his eyes this time and started off down the hall. "What about you, Gerry? Want me to check under your bed?"

"I'll check under my own bed," the older woman said loftily, as if the idea of him going into her bedroom was unspeakably vulgar. "If I find anything amiss, I'll let you know."

"You do that," he muttered.

The door to Camille's bedroom was standing open. He went in and groped around for the light switch, found it and flipped it on. She followed him inside and closed the door. He'd known, of course, that she had something more in mind than getting her closets checked for nonexistent bogeymen. Turning, he brought his hands to his hips. "Let's get this over with."

She stared at him for a moment, seemed to make a decision and folded her arms. "All right. Here it is. I'm worried about my little sister."

"Jillian's safe enough at the moment."

"I'm not talking about Janzen. I'm talking about you."

His hackles instantly rose. "What about me?"

Camille turned and walked over to the bed, then dropped down onto its edge, hands braced against the mattress. "Surely you've noticed that she's developed an interest in you."

What I've noticed is that I've developed an interest in her, he thought. He said, "Oh?"

She kicked her shoes off and lifted her feet to curl them beneath her silk robe. "I'd appreciate it if you wouldn't encourage Jilly. I wouldn't want her to develop unreasonable expectations where you're concerned."

"Unreasonable expectations?" he echoed flatly, appalled at the implication. "You think that for Jillian to expect me to return her interest is unreasonable? Lady, you've got some warped sense of your sister's needs and capabilities."

"I think I know my sister a little better than you do," Camille said reasonably. "I just don't want you to encourage her by paying her too much attention."

"How can you put your sister down like this?" he demanded. "Or am I supposed to be flattered that you're painting me as some unattainable godlike creature that the hopeless little waif dare not approach?"

Camille stared at him for a long moment, her lips twisted into a small smile. "Do you have intentions toward my sister, Zach?"

Intentions. The word fell like a stone through his mind, and he instinctively sidestepped it. "What has that got to do with anything?"

She adjusted the hem of her robe carefully. "Just answer the question. Do you have intentions toward my sister?"

He opened his mouth, then closed it again. His only intention toward Jillian was to keep as much distance between her and him as possible. Not that he'd had much luck at it so far, but he wouldn't give Camille the satisfaction of hearing him say so. He didn't have to. The smugness of her expression told him that much.

"Then I want you to leave her alone," she said evenly.

He just stared at her, making no promises, but in his heart he knew that she was right. Now more than ever he really should stay far, far away from Jillian Waltham. The question was, could he?

Jillian lay in her bed listening for the sound of his footsteps in the hall. What was he doing in Camille's room for so long? No matter how shaken up Camille was, it couldn't take this long for him to put her fears to rest. She saw him standing here in her own room, his arms around her sister, and her stomach turned over. Camille was so pretty. Camille was successful and confident. She was experienced with men, too. She would know how to attract a man, how to fix his interest. Sighing, Jillian closed her eyes and tried not to think about it, but when she finally heard the opening of the door and the sound of muffled footsteps on the carpet, her heart leaped into her throat. She sat up, hoping...hoping... But the footsteps passed right by her door without a pause. Disappointment made her slump over her knees, her hands going to her hair.

Who was she kidding? A man like Zach Keller couldn't seriously be interested in her. True, when he'd first awakened her, she'd been dreaming about that kiss, but then reality had intruded and she'd known something was very wrong. Going into his arms had seemed the most reasonable and right thing to do, but a momentary safety was all he had offered. Perhaps it was all he had ever offered. Yes, she had almost certainly read much too much into his actions.

Collapsing back onto her pillow, she tried to make her mind a blank and find sleep, but long minute after long minute passed, and even relaxation escaped her. It was no use. She wasn't going to sleep any more this night. Sitting up again, she mentally surveyed her options. At the moment she was out of reading material. She'd intended to make a stop by the bookstore on her way home this evening, but the day hadn't exactly gone as planned, not that she was complaining. The only accessible television was in the den, which was where Zach had most likely camped, so that was out. She considered making an entry in the journal that she kept sporadically, but she knew the results would be maudlin at best. No use feeling sorry for herself. Looked like a warm glass of milk was the best solution.

Sighing, she got up and left the room, bothering with neither robe nor slippers, as was her custom. What was the point when her sleep shirt was as decent as any dress and she relished the feel of the floor beneath her feet? Quietly, she slipped into the kitchen and went to the refrigerator, to take out the milk. Leaving the door ajar so she could use the light, she filled a mug and heated it in the microwave, stopping it before it beeped. She added a few drops of vanilla to the warm milk and stirred it in with a spoon. Just as she lifted the mug to her lips, Zach said from the shadows, "Does that really improve the taste?"

She fought down the thrill that skipped over her nerve endings by wrinkling her nose. "Not enough."

"I prefer a good book myself."

She smiled at that. "I didn't get to the bookstore today for some reason."

He chuckled, saying, "Put that down and come in here."

She sat the mug on the counter and followed him into the den, closing the refrigerator door on the way. He had turned on the television but kept the volume way down. The flicker of the screen was the only light in the large, cool room. He motioned toward the couch. "Sit down."

She folded herself onto the powder-blue couch and waited, sensing that something was coming. He put his hands to his hips and looked at her.

"I had a talk with your sister about you."

Relief shimmered through her. So that was why he was in Camille's room so long. She relaxed and curled up her legs, saying, "Oh? What about me?"

He sucked a deep breath through his nostrils and pushed it out again. "Camille thinks I ought to keep away from you."

The relief vanished. "That's silly!"

"No, it isn't." Sighing, he walked over and sat down next to her. "You draw me, Jillian. I'm not sure why, really, but I know it's unwise."

She was dismayed and suddenly a little desperate. "Why would you say such a thing?"

"Listen, please," he said, taking her hands in his. "What I do has the potential of real danger."

"I know that."

He squeezed her hands, signaling that he didn't want her to interrupt. "I realized a long time ago that it wouldn't be fair to ask anyone to share that with me."

"But—"

He dropped her hands, hurrying on. "That's not the only reason I want to stay uninvolved. I like my life. I do important work, and I'm not going to give it up."

"Of course you're not," she said, "but that doesn't mean you can't have relationships."

"Relationships, yes," he said. "But not a *serious* relationship. I won't go through that again."

"So this is really about Serena?" she asked, but he shook his head.

"No, honey, this is about you. I don't want to see you hurt."

"What makes you think I'm going to let you hurt me?" she demanded. "I'm not some helpless little waif who can't take care of herself, no matter what anybody thinks. Just because I don't stomp my feet and shout and demand everything go my way doesn't mean I'm too stupid to make my own decisions and choose my own path."

He blinked at that, obviously surprised by her vehemence. "Okay," he said slowly. "So just exactly what path do you think you're choosing here?"

She frowned, not at all certain now what she wanted, hoped for, from him. She knew only that he made her feel special in a way no one else had, not that she'd had much experience with men. Quite the opposite, in fact. But she knew that she liked the way he made her feel, that she didn't want to stop feeling this way, that it was unfair on some fundamental level to expect it of her. Exactly what she was going to do about it, she didn't know, unless... It would mean taking a chance, a huge chance, but he had kissed her twice now of his own volition. Perhaps it was her turn to take the initiative. She looked down at her hands in her lap, working up her courage. What was the worst that could happen? He was on the verge of forgetting he'd ever known her now. Decision made, she lifted her head. The wavering light cut shadowy vales in the half of his face turned away from the television, limning the strong bone structure of his forehead, nose, chin and jaw. He was a breathtakingly handsome man, even in near darkness, and her heart was beating hard at the audacity of what she was about to do, and yet she found the courage to slide closer on the couch, to lift her hands and place them on the corded slopes of his shoulders, pulling herself against him.

His hands went to her waist, even as he leaned back slightly. "Jillian? Are you sure about this?"

She didn't even know what *this* was, only that she must do something to bind him to her before it was too late. Pushing up on one leg, she leaned into him and put her mouth to his. He pushed lightly at her waist, but she slid her arms around his neck and wound them tight. With a groan, he wrapped his arms around her and sank back onto the couch, its padded arm supporting his head. She lay atop his chest, her legs tangling with his, and reveled in the feel of his hands wandering over her hips and down to her thighs, then back again to cup her and pull her against him. She couldn't miss the evidence of his response and exulted in it even as it frightened her a little. It was so male, so elemental, an incontrovertible fact of life with which she had only passing acquaintance.

In truth, she had never before wanted to deepen her acquaintance with sexual desire. What she knew of Camille's liaisons and those of most of her friends had not inspired any great need to join their ranks. It all seemed so shallow, so quickly dismissed and easily forgotten, that she had never understood the need to take such risks with her person. She had always suspected that for her passion would be more a matter of the heart than the physical, much as it seemed to be with Denise and Worly. They were the only two people she knew who were totally committed to each other. Now she was beginning to understand the danger of allowing one's heart to be engaged in such elemental matters. As much as she wanted Zach, she could not be sure that indulging this mutual passion would gain her anything but heartbreak. Yet what was she to do? Let him walk away without a backward glance?

The hand slowly sliding up beneath her gown did nothing to clear her mind. She gasped, her head spinning, when he slipped it between her legs and rubbed her through her panties. He whorled his tongue around her mouth before breaking the kiss. Shifting and turning her so that she slid down onto the couch and was wedged against the back and the seat, he rose above her on one elbow and trailed his fingertips over her mouth and chin and downward to the slight fullness of one breast. She closed her eyes, amazed that the same breast she had washed, dressed and laid upon for so many years could produce such intense sensation when stroked by another. Would it feel this way with anyone else? She couldn't quite believe that it would.

"I want to make love to you," he whispered, "but I have to be sure that it's what you want, too."

She opened her eyes. "I think it is."

Sighing, he shook his head. "Not good enough, sweetheart." He began to pull away, but she caught him to her.

"Please, Zach. Try to understand. It's just that I've never before...I—I've never wanted to with anyone else."

He studied her face for a long moment before comprehension dawned. When it did, a myriad of emotions flickered across his face, among them shock, dismay, fascination and something surprisingly like respect. "Dear God," he breathed. "What a treasure you are!"

"You don't mind?"

"Mind? Hell, yes. I want you so badly that I'm quite willing to overlook a great many of my own convictions. But not this one. You deserve better than this." He pushed his hand into her hair, cupping her ear in his palm. "You deserve everything, more than I have to offer, I'm afraid."

"Don't say that," she pleaded.

His smile was sad, determined. "Facts are facts, sweetheart. You're much too dear, much too wonderful to settle for what I can give you. I want you to wait for the right man."

"But you—"

"No," he said. "No."

He pulled her face to his chest and wrapped his arms around her, holding on as if he'd never let her go again. She felt perilously close to tears, and she wasn't even certain why. Disappointment was part of it, of course, but also relief. Then again, she was aware of something else, something unfamiliar, not pride exactly and not shame, something in between perhaps and yet totally different. She had thrown herself at him, but it was something she'd never done before and would probably never have the courage to do again, and he admired her for that, which thrilled her. On the other hand, he didn't love her, and he had as good as said that he never could, which was breaking her heart. What was one more difficult fact to face when she'd had so much practice at it, though? As usual, she would take what she could get and be thankful for it; so determined, she swallowed down the tears and returned his embrace, content for the moment to merely hold and be held. Tomorrow she would find a way to be happy again. Tomorrow.

Zach jerked awake, aware of a painful screech somewhere near to hand. Not an alarm clock, surely. Who would want to start his day with such a horrible sound? He attempted to lift his hands to cover his ears and abruptly realized that at least one of his arms was caught beneath something. Something that blew a gust of hot air against his chest and snuggled closer, if that was possible. Jillian. He had no time to consider the situation more fully. The screech had become words.

"You little slut!"

Zach popped his eyes open and glared at the fuzzy form standing over him. Correction, them. Jillian stirred at the same time, and he felt her stiffen against him.

"Gerry!" she gasped.

A hand flashed out. Instinctively, Zach caught it, aware only as his fingers closed around her ropy wrist that it was Gerry who had swung at Jillian. Anger had him surging upward and thrusting that hand back from where it came. "What the hell is going on?"

"That is painfully obvious!" she shrieked, jerking back her hand as though he'd bitten her. She spewed venom at Jillian. "You ungrateful little bi—"

"Hey!" Zach jabbed a finger at her. "What's your problem?"

Gerry's face contorted in pure hatred as she confronted Jillian. "Your sister took you in when no one else in the world would have you!"

Jillian made a helpless sound. "I know that!"

"And this is how you pay her back?" Gerry shook a fist at Zach. "You know she's interested in him! He went into her room with her last night!"

"Hold on!" Zach snapped. "There is absolutely nothing between Camille and me!"

"Because of her!" Gerry screamed. "It's always because of her!"

"That's absurd. Why don't you just calm down and—"

"We fell asleep," Jillian said pleadingly. "Nothing happened. We were just... We fell asleep, that's all."

"Don't, Jillian," Zach said. "You don't owe her any explanations."

"Oh, yes, she does!" Gerry hissed. "She owes me a great deal more than that! And she owes her precious sister everything, just everything!"

"Will you calm down!" Zach demanded, but he might as well have saved his breath.

Gerry balled both hands into fists and hammered her thighs with them, her turban slipping sideways, nightdress and robe twisting around her. "How could you do this again?" she bawled at Jillian. "Wasn't once enough? You have to steal every man she wants?"

Again? Puzzled, Zach fixed his attention on Jillian, whose face had lost every vestige of color. "What's she talking about?"

Jillian shook her head, staring at Gerry. "It's not true," she said weakly. "You know it's not true."

"You stole Janzen from Camille!" Gerry accused. "He was in love with her, and you threw yourself at him until he gave in."

"No!" Jillian exclaimed. "It wasn't like that!" Unable to take in what he was hearing, Zach bounded up off the couch to stare down at her. "It wasn't," she told him, holding up a hand beseechingly.

"Then why did he tell Camille that it was *you* he really loved?" Gerry demanded. "Why did he break up with her and swear the two of you would be together? Why did he threaten her when she told him to stay away from you?"

Stunned, Zach watched as Jillian swallowed painfully, tears glimmering in her eyes. She'd lied to him. Jillian had lied to him. He couldn't believe it. He couldn't *not* believe it. Most of all he couldn't understand why he wasn't angry, why instead it felt as though a hot blade had been driven deep into his chest.

"It wasn't like that," Jillian said to him. "I don't even like Janzen. I never did. When he first started coming on to me, I thought it was another of his tasteless jokes."

"You lie!" Gerry screamed. "You enticed him. He was jealous of Camille's celebrity, and you played on that! You—"

"Mother!"

Zach looked up as Camille swooped into the room, her robe belling around her.

"What on earth are you doing?"

Gerry poked a finger at the couch and Jillian, who knelt there, hugging herself. "They were sleeping together! The two of them, right there!"

Camille glared at Zach, one hand sweeping her hair back from her face. "Didn't I tell you—"

"Not nearly enough," he interrupted. "You've lied to me. All of you. Eibersen isn't after you. He's after Jillian!"

"No," Jillian said, shaking her head. "I told him. I want no part of him. I never did. I told him that!"

Camille lifted her chin and folded her arms. "And he blames me for it," Camille said. "The man has lost his mind. He came to me saying that he was hopelessly in love with Jillian, and naturally I forbade him any contact with her."

"I don't *want* any contact with him," Jillian insisted softly.

"He believes I've turned her against him," Camille went on as Jillian hadn't spoken. "He says I've made her choose, and he wants to punish me for it. So, you see, no one really lied. I'm the one he's angry with, the one he's obsessed with."

"The poem he spray-painted all over your kitchen," Zach said numbly. "That wasn't for you. It was a love poem, albeit a bad one, for her." He nodded at Jillian. "And the window he painted—that was hers, too." Suddenly, his head began to throb. He pressed his fingertips to his temples, feeling the blood vessels beneath the skin expand.

"It's all her fault!" Gerry cried, pointing a finger at Jillian.

"Cut it out," Zach muttered, massaging his temples as the throbbing in his head grew more pronounced.

"She's not the sweet, naive little sister you've always wanted her to be," Gerry told Camille. "It's her, I tell you."

"Mother, that's enough!" Camille ordered sternly. Regally, she lifted her chin, her gaze challenging Zach somehow.

Suddenly he saw it, the insecurity, the uncertainty of a little girl whose father had abandoned her along with her mother for someone he loved more. She had to believe she was Eibersen's target. She couldn't bear to believe that her former lover might actually be fixated on her innocent little sister instead of her. For the first time Zach felt sorry for her. The poor, deluded thing would always come in second to Jillian. And she knew it. She fought it, but deep inside, she knew it. As for Jillian, right now he couldn't even think beyond the fact that she'd lied to him. All he could think was that he needed some space here, some objectivity. He looked at Jillian and remembered how dangerously close he'd come to making love to her last night, how dangerously close he was to losing his heart even now, knowing that she'd lied to him.

"I have to go," he muttered, pinching the bridge of his nose.

"What about the new security code?" Camille asked shrilly.

Security code. Five digits. He tried to think and finally pulled down the most obvious numbers. "Um, use this. Nine, two, seven, six, seven. Got that? Nine, twenty-seven, sixty-seven. I'll, um, call it in on my way home."

"Nine, two, seven, six, seven," Camille repeated. She smiled mockingly. "What's that, your birthday?"

"Yeah. But Eibersen won't know that." He couldn't make himself look at Jillian. He didn't have to see her face to know she was crying, but he couldn't do anything about that. He was having enough trouble holding himself together at the moment. "I'll, uh, be in touch," he muttered, and then he turned around and walked away, uncomfortably aware that it was very likely the most cowardly thing he'd ever done in his life but completely unable to stop himself. She had lied to him, and the ache of it told him how disastrously close he was to losing something essential to his well-being—his heart.

Jillian listened to the sound of the door closing and knew one of the bleakest, loneliest moments of her life. Why had she lied to him? Why hadn't she told him everything from the beginning? Camille wouldn't even have had to know, but she hadn't even thought of that. She'd thought only of doing what Camille wanted, of protecting Camille both emotionally and physically— for all the good it had done. The look in Camille's eyes was colder and harder than any other she had ever seen before.

"Well," she said, as if confirming Jillian's worst fears, "you've really done it this time. I doubt he'll even continue working for us now."

Jillian wiped her face with her hands and shook her head. "He's not like that. Zach is genuinely good. He'll be here if we need him."

Camille chuckled scathingly. "Good grief, Jill, are you that naive? Just because he slept with you doesn't mean that he's Prince Charming in blue jeans! In fact, it means just the opposite. That man took advantage of you, and after I expressly forbade it! We'll be lucky if we ever hear from him again! He'll have his office bill us, and that will be that!''

"But he didn't take advantage of me,'' Jillian protested.

"No doubt!'' Gerry said with a snort. "It was probably the other way around.''

Jillian felt a sense of resolve, like a small, cold chunk of steel in the pit of her stomach that slowly expanded to fill her chest. She sat back on her heels. "As a matter of fact, you're right,'' she said evenly. "He didn't come to me. I came to him. And he turned me down.'' The hitch in her voice caught her unaware, and with it came a tiny crack in the armor of her resolve. Hurt and embarrassment flowed through. She bit her lip, head bowed.

"I knew it!'' Gerry was crowing. "She threw herself at him! She admitted it.''

Camille's voice, when she finally spoke, was as chilly as an Arctic blast. "Is that right, Jilly? Is that what happened? You threw yourself at him?''

Jillian swallowed, a profound sadness beginning to overwhelm all else. "I asked him to make love to me. He refused.''

"And you did the same thing with Janzen!'' Gerry accused. "Admit it!''

"No.'' Jillian raised her head to look her sister straight in the eye. "I never approached Janzen. Never. He came on to me, and I sent him away—repeatedly. I wanted nothing to do with him, ever. You know that.''

"Do I?'' Camille asked, and the very last vestige of hope to which Jillian had clung evaporated. "You must have done something,'' Camille went on cattily. "I see that clearly now. He would never have just chosen you over me. It doesn't make sense, but I wouldn't believe you could betray me that way.''

"Betray you?'' Jillian exclaimed. "Is that what you really think?'' But it was, of course. She could see it in Camille's eyes, the desperate, deliberate belief. "Dear heaven,'' Jillian whispered. "You would really rather believe that I *stole* him from you than that he might actually *prefer* me to you. Are you that insecure?''

"Don't be stupid!" Camille snapped.

"How dare you?" Gerry huffed at the same time.

Jillian closed her eyes, knowing that nothing would ever be the same now. She could no longer delude herself, no longer hold on to the vague idea that if only she was good enough, quiet enough, meek enough, helpful enough, plain enough, Camille might actually love her. She had indeed been used, but not by Zach, not even by Janzen, at least not compared with how her own sister had used her. It hit her, almost humorously, that Zach had been right all along. He'd pegged Camille right from the beginning, and her, too. From the very first he'd seen her for exactly what she was, needy, alone, pathetic. She'd have laughed if it hadn't been so sad, so heartbreaking.

Slowly, she unwound her legs and got up off the couch. "I'll leave right away," she said softly.

"Leave?" Camille echoed. "And just where do you think you'll go?"

"I don't know," Jillian said. "It doesn't matter."

Gerry scoffed. "Doesn't matter?"

"Not anymore," Jillian said dispiritedly. "Not anymore." She walked around Gerry and Camille, her legs seeming to weigh twice what they should, but she would not waver now. This was, in fact, long overdue. She wasn't a child who needed someone to protect her anymore; she was an adult, at least as sensible as most. What had happened right here in this very room last night told her that. She had never offered herself to Janzen Eibersen, despite what Camille chose to think, and she never would, no matter how lonely and desperate she might be. The only man to whom she had ever offered herself was the only one decent enough to turn her down, and she found reason to be proud in that. Yes, it was time. And she would be fine on her own. She would be just fine, and if not, she would still be better off away from here—whatever happened.

* * *

Jillian groaned and rolled over on the lumpy, dusty couch, trying to find a comfortable position.

"How long do you think you can keep this up?" Denise asked, and Jillian slit her eyelids open just a tad. It was enough to blind her, the sunshine pouring through the windows slicing into her head like splinters of glass. She squeezed her eyes shut again, sighing.

"I'll find someplace else to go," she said groggily.

"That's not what I meant, and you know it," Denise said, wedging her butt onto the edge of the couch next to Jillian. "Let me get a bed in here. We can curtain off one end of the room and—"

"No," Jillian said, pushing up into a sitting position. She blinked against the glare and lifted her arms, trying to stretch out the kinks in her shoulders and spine. "I'm fine here for now. I'll find a permanent place soon. I just need a roommate to share the expenses."

Denise studied her for a moment, then shook her head. "I still can't believe she threw you out."

"Camille didn't throw me out," Jillian insisted for the dozenth time. "I told you. I made the decision myself."

"And about time, too," Denise pointed out. "But why now? She's been jerking you around for years."

"It doesn't matter," Jillian muttered. "It's done, and it's for the best. I won't be going back."

Denise studied her a moment longer, then abruptly nodded. "Right. Okay. Well, at least you're getting a lot of work done. The piece is looking great, by the way. Even Worly says so."

Jillian smiled. "Thanks." She yawned, pushing her hands through her hair. "I have to get going. Don't want to be late for work."

Denise got up off the couch and reached for the light blanket that Jillian had kicked off. "How's that going by the way?"

"Work?" Jillian shrugged. Every day at the deli was pretty much like the last, especially since Zach had made himself scarce. She couldn't really blame him. No one liked to be lied to, especially when he was trying to help. She sighed, wondering how she could have screwed up any more. Not only had she kept the truth from him, she'd thrown herself at him in every way she could manage, not to mention ruining his stakeout by letting Janzen get a look at her. She was convinced now that was how it had happened. What else could it have been? And then to have Gerry find them together like that, make all those baseless accusations. She winced at the very thought of it. "Work's fine," she said belatedly.

Denise just looked at her and began folding the blanket. When she was finished, not one corner was squared with another, and Jillian had to smile. That seemed to reassure Denise somehow. She visibly relaxed and tossed aside the blanket. "Want some breakfast?"

Jillian subdued the urge to wrinkle her nose. Cold pizza was Denise's breakfast of choice. And lunch. And dinner. And... "Sure," Jillian said enthusiastically, bouncing up. "Why not?" It was then that her gaze fell on the letter lying on the floor just inside the front door, obviously having been slipped through the mail slot. But the mail didn't come until late in the afternoon, and even at a distance she could see that this particular envelope bore no stamp. A shiver of foreboding seized her, and suddenly she saw a picture of Zach Keller's face, but it was too late for that. Too late.

Lois tapped on the door, then opened it and stuck her head inside the room. "Got a minute, Boss?"

Zach tamped down his irritation. Lately, everything irritated him. Living irritated him. He put down the tape recorder into which he had been speaking and tossed aside the case file. Leaning back, he waved her into the room. She slipped inside and closed the door behind her, a sure sign that someone waited in the outer office. "What's up?"

"I've got a guy out here who wants to see you. Name's Whirly or some such thing."

"Never heard of him. What's it about?"

"The Waltham case."

Zach mentally recoiled. "There is no Waltham case." After

two weeks of complete calm, Camille had called, four days ago now, to tell him that Janzen Eibersen had taken a job out of state. In her estimation, the whole fiasco was behind her and his services were no longer needed. He had his sources confirm what her sources had told her. Eibersen had indeed taken a job with a radio station in Juneau, Alaska. He didn't have to go, of course, and even if he did, he wasn't due to report there for sixty days, but Camille seemed to think that didn't matter. Zach hadn't argued with her. He hadn't dared. Now this. "Tell him I'm busy."

The door opened behind Lois and a ghoul slipped inside. "I ain't going nowhere till you hear me out, dude." He was tall and skinny, with long, lank hair dyed ink black and a silver nose ring. Folding his tattooed arms over a black leather vest, he struck a belligerent pose.

Zach sighed. "Listen, whoever you are—"

"Name's Worly," the man said stubbornly, stepping forward and sticking out his hand.

Worly. Denise's Worly. Jillian's Denise. The hairs lifted on the back of Zach's neck. Rising slightly, he nodded Worly toward a chair and waved Lois out of the room. She backed up to the door and folded her arms much as Worly had done a moment earlier.

"If this is about Jilly," she said, "I want to hear it."

Resigned, Zach dropped back into his chair and nodded. "Sit down, Mr.—"

"Just 'Worly,' dude. You know, like, just 'Worly.'"

"Sit down, Worly."

Worly dropped into the same chair Jillian had chosen, sprawling as though his bones had suddenly turned to liquid.

"What's on your mind?"

Worly crossed one leg over the other and picked at the toe of his rope sandal. "It started nearly a week ago. First it was a letter. She didn't let us read it, but—"

"She?"

"Jilly, man. She got this letter from Eibersen, and I could tell it scared her, you know, because he knows now where she is."

Zach sat up straight at that. "You're telling me she's left her sister's?"

"Weeks ago."

He almost came out of his chair. "Where is she?"

"She's been crashing on my couch, camping out, you know, and, dude, it can't be too comfortable. We picked that thing up off the side of the road, just off Jefferson, you know, over on the other side of—"

Zach leaned forward, arms spread across the top of his desk. "What about this letter?"

"Not just one, dude," Worly said. "Every day there's like four or five, and they don't come through the mail, you know, like normal stuff. We find 'em all over, in the cars, taped to the door, inside these weird packages."

"Packages?"

"Weird stuff. Knives and nails, broken bits of glass, cans of spray paint. He writes these stupid poems and says crap like, 'Why don't you just cut my heart out?' and 'What's it gonna take to make you love me?' I don't like the sound of any of it, man. I think he's building up to something."

Zach reined in a growing sense of alarm. "I'm told he's taken a job in Alaska."

"Yeah, he keeps writing about that, saying how they can start a new life together there, and he says he ain't going without her. I don't think she's safe. I mean, dude, I came home late last night from a gig, you know, and like, the front door's standing open, and there's this box sitting right at the foot of the couch where she's sleeping, and it's, like, actually *ticking*, you know. I thought it was a bomb, swear to God! It was this ugly clock, all battered and beat-up, and this note says, 'Time's running out.' I don't like it, man. I just don't like it. She's not safe. We gotta do something."

Zach nodded and rubbed his hands over his thighs. His blood had run cold when Worly had mentioned the door standing open. Eibersen clearly had gone inside the apartment to leave his little package, but would he be content with that next time? He wouldn't be the first man to think of rape as a kind of seduction.

"You have to get her out of there," he said. "Eibersen's already demonstrated that he can get to her."

"Don't I know it, man, but where's she gonna go? Back to her sister's? I don't think so. She's trying to scrape up the money to get a place of her own, you know, even got that old jalopy of hers for sale, but, dude, it ain't worth the price of the rubber on it now, and at that, those tires are bald. B-A-L-D, man. Slick."

Zach got the point only too well. Jillian needed someplace safe to go until Eibersen either left town or could be properly discouraged, but her options were limited, and at the moment he was blank himself. "I'll think of something. I don't know what, yet, but something."

"She could have stayed with me," Lois said, speaking up for the first time. She'd been so quiet Zach had forgotten she was there.

He nodded with relief. "That might work."

"I said, 'could have,'" she pointed out. "My daughter and her kids moved in with me after her divorce last month, if you remember."

"Oh. Right." Crestfallen, he pushed his hand through his hair. "I don't suppose even temporarily..."

"I wish. We're four people in a two-bedroom apartment now. My grandson's sleeping on the couch as it is. In a few more months, maybe, when my daughter's back on her feet..."

"No way," Worly said, shaking his snaky hair. "This dude's not waiting months to make his big move. I can feel it, man."

"You're right," Zach agreed. "She needs a safe place now."

"Your apartment building is like a fortress," Lois noted.

Not that he hadn't already thought it himself. "That's true," he said. "But my deed has more restrictions than an arms control pact."

"There are ways around restrictions," Lois said slyly. "You could tell them she's your sister."

"Which would buy us all of a week," he said dismissively. "Hell, if she was my *wife,* I couldn't get her in longer than that without submitting in writing a request to have my lease altered."

"Well, hey, dude, that's the perfect solution, then, isn't it?"

Worly said, sitting up straight. "I mean, you could just, like, tell them she's your wife, right?"

Zach's heart thumped once and stopped. "I—it's not quite that simple. I'd have to, um, submit papers."

"Like a marriage license," Lois said, coming closer to the desk. "They aren't hard to get, you know. You just have to apply."

How had he known she was going to say that? Why had he thought it himself? He gulped. "I—I'm not sure that's smart. What I mean is, I couldn't... That is..."

"For goodness' sake, Boss, haven't you ever heard of a marriage of convenience? You know what an annulment is? A divorce, even."

Zach sliced a hand through the air. "I'm not hearing this!" He got up from his chair and turned toward the window, hands at his hips. "Just let me think, will you?"

"Hey," Worly said, "whatever. Just do it fast, man. I've got another gig tonight, and I don't like the notion of her being at the loft alone."

Zach stared out the window a long moment. His apartment would be the safest possible place for Jillian, but could he bear to have her that close, even for just a week? Maybe he had no choice. Maybe somehow he never had. He shook his head and turned.

"Lois, I want you to get in touch with that psychiatrist we consulted with on the Michaelson case. Shorter, I think his name is. I want info on obsessive fixations. Then call Gabler and tell him to get back on Eibersen. I want him watched every minute. I'll go downstairs and talk to Jillian in a little while." He looked at Worly, an unlikely hero at best, and actually felt himself smile. "Whatever else happens, I can promise you that she won't be alone at your apartment anymore, if I have to stand guard myself."

Worly unfolded himself from the chair, swept back his freaky hair and wobbled his head in a nod. "Cool," he said and stuck out his hand. "My old lady said you was the man."

Zach came forward to give that hand a hearty shake. "I don't know about that, but thanks for coming in. You did the right thing.''

"No sweat, man. Gotta protect our Jilly girl. I mean, who else has she got, right?"

Who else, indeed? He couldn't tell this character how desperately he wished that she did have someone else, anyone else, but him.

Chapter Seven

Zach hung up the phone and frowned down at the notes he'd taken. Dr. Shorter had generously given his lunch hour to listen to Zach's tale of Janzen Eibersen and answer his questions. Zach only wished the information was more encouraging. Part of him wanted to let Jillian go, to believe, even, that she deserved these difficulties for having lied to him, but in his heart of hearts he knew that she'd only been trying to protect her sister's vaunted ego. He doubted that she'd even understood that she was in as much—or more—danger as Camille. Heck, she probably still didn't understand how precarious her situation was. The question now was, what to do about it? He knew what the next step had to be, and he'd put it off as long as he could, but no more. It was time to talk to Jillian.

He pushed back his chair, got up and reached for his jacket, but before he could get both arms in the sleeves, his cell phone rang. He paused long enough to unclip it from his waist, extend the antenna and turn it on. "Yeah?"

It was Gabler, the operative he'd sent to find Janzen Eibersen. "He's in the building!"

"What?"

"He's in your building! He's coming after you, man!"

"Me?"

"Who else?"

Zach knew who else. He flew out of the office, his jacket trailing by one arm, and tore past Lois's desk. "What's wrong?"

"Stay here!" he shouted, running for the elevator, the phone gripped in his hand. He punched the button and waited frantically for the car to come and the doors to open, fighting the impulse to take the stairs, which would, ultimately, be slower. "Gabler?" he shouted into the phone, hoping Gabe could get to Jillian more quickly than he could, but the other man had broken the connection. Zach punched off the phone as he stepped into the elevator, which was blessedly empty. Someone on a lower floor signaled, however, and the car slowed again immediately after taking off. Zach hit the wall with his fist in a panic of impatience as the car came to a stop and the doors slid open. Ruthlessly, Zach punched the door closed again, leaving a middle-aged man in a starched white shirt and suspenders gaping in confusion. The elevator car dropped straight to the lobby this time. Zach managed to clip his phone to his belt once more and get his jacket on properly before the elevator touched down. Squeezing through the doors while they were still opening, he sprinted across the marble floor toward the deli.

He knew something was unfolding even before he got there because a crowd had gathered in front of the deli counter. Shouldering his way through, he drew up right next to Gabler, who looked decidedly out of place in his garage mechanic coveralls and ball cap. Jillian was plastered against the glass case, a look of horror on her piquant face as Janzen Eibersen gazed up at her from one knee. He was wearing a pin-striped suit and a pale-blue shirt with a banded collar. On his open palm lay a gold ring sporting a solitaire diamond.

"So, Jillian," Eibersen was saying, "will you marry me?"

Jillian stared. "No! Why would you think—"

Eibersen lurched up and grabbed her left hand, trying to cram the ring onto her finger. "You have to marry me! You know I love you!"

Jillian tugged at her hand. "Stop it!"

"But you left Camille's! That means you chose me over her!"

Zach shook off his momentary shock and stepped forward. "Jillian."

The look of relief that swept over her when she saw him there pierced his heart. She tugged her hand free of Eibersen's and reached for him. "Zach!" He literally pulled her across the small space at the center of the crowd and into his arms. A buzz of whispered comments went up. He ignored it, concentrating on Eibersen as the other man's curiosity gave way to outrage.

"Get away from him!" Eibersen demanded, reaching out. Jillian skittered away, arms sliding around Zach.

"No! I won't marry you!"

"Jillian, come here!" Eibersen shouted, reaching around Zach to snatch her wrist.

Rage seared Zach. He grabbed Eibersen by the throat and shoved him back. The other man stumbled against the deli case, knocking off a domed plastic container of cheese cubes. From the corner of his eye, Zach saw the manager dart around the counter and through a door. No doubt he'd be explaining himself to the police soon, maybe one of his own brothers. So be it.

"Touch her again and I'll break your arms," he told Eibersen flatly.

Straightening and sweeping his hair out of his face, Eibersen demanded, "Who the hell are you?"

Jillian crept to Zach's side, one arm still loosely wrapped around his waist. Zach knew what he had to say and do. It was the perfect solution. He shifted her behind him again and lifted his chin in challenge. "I'm the reason she won't be marrying you."

Eibersen surged forward, getting right in Zach's face, eyes maniacally wide in an attempt to salvage his pride and intimidate Zach. "What makes you think you have anything to say about it?"

Zach tugged Jillian's arm away and stepped forward, toe-to-toe with Eibersen. "It's simple," he said calmly. "Jillian is marrying me."

Someone gasped—several someones, actually. Eibersen reeled backward, his gaze skittering around wildly until he found Jillian, peering around Zach's shoulder.

"It's a lie!"

Zach reached back and laid a hand on Jillian's slender thigh, cautioning her to let him do the talking. "The lady's marrying me."

"I don't believe it!"

"Too bad."

"When?" Eibersen sneered, desperate now and badly shaken. "What's the date?"

"Right away," Zach said. "Before the end of the week."

Eibersen shook his head, his straight, pale hair sliding around his face. He reached out a hand to Jillian. "No. Jilly, you can't! You're supposed to be with *me!* Tell him!"

Zach turned slightly and slid an arm around Jillian's shoulders, encouraging her with a direct look to go along with this. He could see the shock and confusion in her big blue eyes and something else, too, something that made him want to drag her off to the closest cave, something that also made him want to run fast in the opposite direction. After a moment, she looked away and addressed herself to Eibersen.

"I'm sorry, Jan," she said softly but firmly. "I just don't love you."

"You're saying you love him?" Eibersen demanded.

She hesitated, and it felt as though a fist reached inside Zach's chest and squeezed his heart. Finally, she said, "Yes."

A smattering of applause broke out among her co-workers.

Something ugly and frightening contorted Eibersen's face. He clutched the ring in his fist and shook it at Zach. "You can't do this!"

"It's done," Zach said flatly. The fist in his chest had turned into a block of ice. Eibersen abruptly shoved his way through the crowd and stormed off. Zach turned, watching Eibersen all the way out of the building, only dimly aware of the congratulations being poured over him until Gabler himself pounded him on the back.

"Hey, man, this is great! I had no idea!"

"Neither did I," Zach muttered, then he poked Gabe in the shoulder. "Hey, get after him, and don't let him out of your sight." Gabler nodded and started away. "And Gabe."

"Yeah?"

"Thanks."

Gabler grinned, displaying a gap in his teeth, and waved a beefy hand in acknowledgment before hurrying off. Suddenly Jillian shrugged off his loose embrace and hissed at him, "What's going on? Who was that?"

Zach looked down at her, painfully aware of the crowd still milling about them. He tried to keep his voice normal and only managed to leach it of expression. "That's Gabler. He works for me sometimes."

She frowned at Gabler's rapidly retreating back. "Why's he wearing that outfit?"

It seemed a perfectly stupid question to ask at the moment, and he found himself snapping, "It's a disguise. He was following Eibersen."

Comprehension dawned in those enormous eyes. "Oh." She looked down self-consciously then, seeming to draw in on herself.

Inexplicably irritated, he said roughly, "We need to talk." Nodding shyly, she ran a hand up the opposite arm as if chilled. Zach found it a frighteningly erotic gesture. Gulping, he grabbed that hand and yanked on it, towing her toward the elevators at a determined clip.

"Someone cover the counter for me!" she called over her shoulder.

A chorus of encouragement told them both that they need not worry on that score, that they could take all the time they needed as far as her co-workers were concerned, but those silly women couldn't know, as Zach did, that she wouldn't be back, not until Eibersen was gone for good. And maybe not then. Maybe never. Unless... Suddenly he knew what was bothering him. Somewhere deep inside him he had expected her to throw herself into his arms and squeal with delight. He had expected kisses and declarations of genuine love. He had expected to have to set her straight, to explain that the marriage thing was a ploy, a means of protecting her. Apparently he'd expected too much, and now he had to wonder how he was going to protect himself.

She had almost believed it. Almost. When he'd first shown up, she'd wanted to throw herself at him, but she didn't know if he was there for her or not. He could have been coming down for a cup of coffee. He could have been on his way out. But then he had reached for her, and she had gladly gone to him. Now she realized that Camille was probably still paying him to keep an eye on her. It was all part of the job, and he was obviously regretting it now. He wouldn't even look at her, dropping her hand the instant they were out of sight of the others.

"We'll go up to my office," he said, but further conversation was forestalled by two businessmen who got on the elevator with them. Zach managed to get both of them between him and her, and when the two got off several floors below his, he kept to his side of the car as if glued in place. Did he think that she was going to try to hold him to his marriage proposal, if that's what it was?

Determinedly, she put on a smile and thanked him. "That was a masterful stroke of strategy back there. I'm sure Janzen will back off now that he thinks I'm unavailable."

Zach grimaced and pushed his hands through his hair. "I'm not so sure I've done either one of us a favor. Dr. Shorter says these obsessive types sometimes thrive on obstacles, and I certainly gave him another one just now."

"Who's Dr. Shorter?"

He looked at her then, a sharp glance rife with uncertainty. "He's a psychiatrist I sometimes consult with."

The elevator slid to a smooth stop just then, and the doors opened. Zach blocked them with one hand and nodded for her to exit ahead of him. Jillian stepped out into the hallway and turned toward the office. Lois looked up and covered her heart with one hand when they walked in.

"Thank God! What on earth happened?"

Half hoping to divert herself from her own disappointment and half wanting to reassure her friend, Jillian launched into a narrative, telling how Janzen had breezed into the deli, hauled Jillian out from behind the counter, demanded everyone's attention and gone down on one knee to make his absurd marriage proposal, despite her attempts to get rid of him. Then, she said, Zach had arrived and taken care of everything. Not content with that paltry explanation, Lois demanded details from Zach, interrupting to offer fervent thanks that he had put Gabler on Eibersen's trail again. When they came to the part about Zach claiming that he and Jillian were getting married, Lois literally whooped.

"I knew it! I knew it!" She bounced around the room dispensing hugs and smacking kisses as if the engagement were a real one. Zach turned six shades of red and finally escaped into his office. Jillian stayed behind a moment longer to calm Lois and insist that the engagement was for "show and protection only."

"Bull hockey," Lois insisted delightedly. "That man has marriage on his mind."

Afraid to get her hopes up, Jillian shook her head. "No, I'm sure it's all an act."

"Is that what he's told you?"

"Not yet, but I can tell. It's the only thing that makes sense. I haven't even spoken to him in weeks."

"Well, get in there and make up for it now," Lois insisted, pushing her toward the office door. "Go on. I'm betting he goes through with it."

"Don't delude yourself," Jillian said. "Zach's not in love with me."

"You're certain of that?"

Jillian shrugged. "Let's put it this way, the last time I saw him, I literally threw myself at him, and he more of less patted me on the head and told me to go to sleep, which I did. Then the next morning my half sister's mom came in and found us there and—"

"Us?"

"Zach and me, but nothing happened. We just fell asleep."

"Together?"

"But nothing happened," Jillian repeated.

Lois lifted an eyebrow skeptically. "Just go along with it," she advised. "See what develops."

Jillian smiled doubtfully. "Don't say I didn't warn you." With that, she went on into the office and closed the door behind her.

Zach was on the phone. He waved her into a chair and turned his back, leaning against the edge of his desk. After a few minutes he sat down and began taking notes. Finally, he rang off, sat back and sighed. "That was Dr. Shorter."

"What did he say?"

"He said it's a toss-up. It depends on how disturbed Eibersen is. Some obsessives get frustrated and go away. Others feel betrayed by their targets and set out to punish them."

Jillian nodded, a lump forming in the center of her chest. "Do you think Janzen is so disturbed that he'll try to harm me?"

Zach pinched the bridge of his nose. "I don't know. Was he punishing Camille before for standing in his way, or simply courting you in his own bizarre fashion?"

Jillian bit her lip. "I can't honestly say. My fear was that he was punishing Camille for telling him to stay away from me. I honestly didn't think that he was that interested in me, just angry at being thwarted."

"You always put Camille first, don't you?" Zach asked softly.

Jillian shook her head. "Not anymore. I guess I thought that was the way to ensure my place in her life, but then that morning when we...when Gerry...well, you know."

"Started making mountains out of molehills," he supplied glumly.

Jillian nodded. "Anyway, I realized it was hopeless."

"What happened that morning, Jillian? What made you leave there?"

She didn't bother asking how he knew she'd moved out. No doubt Camille had informed him. "You heard most of it. Gerry accused me of 'going after you,' as she put it, because Camille had expressed some interest in you. I guess I expected Camille to defend me, but she didn't. I realized then that she couldn't.

She had to blame me. It's how she copes. I just decided I'd had enough. So I left.''

"I shouldn't have left you there on your own. I'm sorry."

She looked up in surprise at that. "It wasn't your fault. Besides, it's for the best. Now that I've had a little distance from the situation, I know that I was trying to earn what has to be given. Anyway, I should be the one apologizing. I should have told you everything from the very beginning."

"Why didn't you?"

She felt incredibly stupid, but she told him the truth. "Camille didn't want anyone to know. She said her image would suffer if it got out that her fiancé left her bed night after night to hit on her goofy little sister."

"That's why you moved into the maid's room, isn't it? To make yourself less available to Eibersen."

Jillian nodded. "The maid's room has a bolt and chain on the door, and it's on the other side of the house."

"Eibersen knew you were sleeping there, didn't he? That's why he painted that particular window."

"I guess so. I don't really understand why Janzen does anything. I've told him over and over again that I want nothing to do with him, but he just doesn't seem to hear it. Maybe now he'll leave me alone."

Zach didn't look convinced, but before he could say anything more, raised voices were heard in the outer office. Jillian turned, recognizing her sister's tones. "What on earth is she doing here?"

Just then the door thrust open, and Camille strode into the room, Lois hot on her heels and crying, "You can't just barge in there!"

"Oh, can't I?" Camille huffed, planting herself at the corner of the desk. She dismissed Lois with a sharp nod of her head and divided a glare between Jillian and Zach, then came back to Jillian to demand, "Have you lost your mind? Your boss just called me to report that you've been staging the most ridiculous scenes in public! What were you thinking?"

Zach was already on his feet. "You've got it backward, as usual. It was Eibersen who—"

Jillian cut him off with a jerk of her hand as she launched to her feet. Had she heard right? "Called you to *report?* Is that what you said? My boss called you to *report* on me?"

Camille folded her arms implacably, the way she ignored the mussed line of her princess seam dress, proclaiming just how upset she was. "Why shouldn't he? I got you that job, after all. What you do there reflects on me!"

It was just the last straw. "*Got* me the job?" Jillian echoed, hurt and angry. "More like you bullied me into the job, just like the one before."

"Well, someone had to," Camille snapped. "You'd starve to death left to your own devices. You don't really think your so called 'artwork' is going to pay the bills, do you?"

"That's beside the point."

"Is it? You were baby-sitting for cash before I pushed you to take the job as receptionist at the studio front desk."

"And then you made me quit that job and come here," Jillian pointed out.

"I had to after Janzen tried to drive his car through the front of the building!" Camille exclaimed.

"So no one would know that he was trying to get to *me* instead of you," Jillian accused.

"It was your own fault!" Camille retorted, throwing up her hands. "You led him on."

"I did not!"

"Then why did he fixate on you?" Camille demanded.

"Maybe because *you* treated him so badly," Jillian shouted.

Camille reeled, her face contorting with outrage. "That's a lie!"

"Is it?" Jillian asked. "I was there, Camille. You bullied and belittled him just like you bully and belittle everyone else. I felt sorry for him, and he must have taken it for more than that."

Camille's eyes had widened almost fearfully, but then she visibly calmed herself, tugging at the line of her dress and darting glances at Zach. "You've twisted everything, Jillian, but then, you never did have a very good grasp on reality. You don't even seem to understand that you're in danger. Janzen doesn't love you, Jillian. He's obsessed with you."

"I know that," Jillian said quietly.

Camille lifted her chin in satisfaction. "All right. Well, you'd better come back home now. We'll just overlook this nonsense as we always have."

Jillian almost laughed. "No, thank you."

"But Jan's going to be after you again. You know how he is."

"I don't care. I won't go back to that house with you, Camille. It's never been my home, no matter how hard I tried to make it so," Jillian said sadly.

Camille was obviously puzzled. "That's nonsense. I made it your home despite Mother's—"

"Gerry doesn't have anything to do with it," Jillian told her. "You're the reason I won't go, Camille. I'm sick and tired of being used."

"Used?" Camille cried laughingly. "How have I used you?"

"Household drudge, chef, gopher, you name it. But most of all, you've fed your ego off me, Camille, and I've let you. But no more."

"This is absurd!"

"Absurd or not, I won't go back to that house with you. I won't go back to being your doormat in the hopes that'll you come to love me."

"Such dramatics!" Camille chided. "And after everything I've done for you!"

Jillian sighed. It was no use. It never had been. "Just go away, Camille. Just leave me alone."

For a moment Camille didn't seem to know what to say, but finally she reverted to big-sisterish disdain. "You're being incredibly foolish, Jillian. Denise and Worly can't protect you."

"But I can," Zach said, both hands going to his waist.

"You don't have anything to say about this!" Camille snapped. "I fired you days ago."

Jillian's head whipped around at that. "What?"

Zach ignored her. "You fired me," he said to Camille, "but Jillian didn't."

"Jillian can't afford to hire you."

"She doesn't have to," Zach said, "because she's going to marry me."

Camille's mouth dropped open, a look of horror on her face, but then she laughed. "You aren't going to marry her!"

"Is that so?" Zach muttered dangerously, but Camille seemed oblivious to his tone.

Jillian shook her head, trying simultaneously to clear it and warn her sister, as Camille said, "You know it is. Jillian told Mother and me that you wouldn't have her even after she threw herself at your head."

Jillian groaned, humiliated beyond endurance. "Camille, please—"

"You think I didn't sleep with her because I didn't want to?" Zach asked incredulously. Jillian put her hands to her face, wishing the floor would open and swallow her whole. "Maybe you think I didn't make love to her because I prefer you? Well, let me tell you, I don't! I didn't sleep with Jillian because I respect her too much to have her first time be some hurried, desperate—"

"Zach!" Jillian pleaded, dropping her hands.

He clamped his jaw shut, and Jillian closed her eyes in relief, only to open them again when Camille said angrily, "I never invited you into my bed, Keller, but if I had, you'd have fallen all over yourself getting there!"

He laughed at her, literally laughed, and shook his head. Jillian braced herself for an eruption. Camille's face pulsed dark red, but then she turned a venomous glare on Jillian.

"Don't you think marrying the pathetic little orphan is carrying the heroics just a tad too far, even for you, Zachary?"

Jillian held her breath, determined not to let Camille see that she was hurt.

Zach leaned forward, both hands flat against the top of his desk. "For your information, I care very much for your sister, and she's not a pathetic little anything."

Suddenly Lois poked Jillian in the ribs from behind and chor-
tled, "Told you so!" Jillian jumped a foot, having forgotten the
woman was still in the room.

Camille frowned furiously at the secretary, who just chuckled.
Tossing her head, Camille targeted Zach once more. "I don't
believe you'll go through with it."

Studiously not looking at Jillian, whose own heart was in her
throat, Zach said evenly, "Believe what you like, but we are
getting married—just as soon as possible."

"I'll call the license bureau," Lois said gleefully, exiting the
room.

Camille rounded on Jillian then. "I forbid this...this...
stupidity!"

"*You* have nothing to say about it," Zach told her firmly.
"Does she, Jillian?" For a moment Jillian could only stare at
him helplessly. "*Does she, Jillian?*"

Abruptly Jillian shook her head, uncertain what was happening, really, all of a sudden exhausted by the whole thing. Camille
ranted and raved a few moments longer, but Jillian couldn't quite
pay her the attention she required, so she finally gave it up,
storming out of the room with the declaration that they shouldn't
bother inviting her to the ceremony because she wouldn't be
lending her consequence to such insanity. Numbly, Jillian
watched her go, then turned back to find Zach sitting at the desk
with both elbows on the blotter and his head in his hands. After
a long moment, she decided that she'd better sit down, too, and
slowly sank into her own chair.

"You don't have to go through with it, you know," she said
softly, praying that he'd look up and declare with heartfelt sincerity that he wanted nothing more than to spend the rest of his
life with her.

Instead, he took a deep breath as if fortifying himself and said,
"Yes, I do. You're right not to go back to Camille's, and I can't
let you go back to that loft." He raised his head then and smiled
wryly. "Worly came to see me this morning, you know, to tell
me what's been going on, and he's right to be concerned. Besides, you could be putting them in danger, too."

Fighting back bitter disappointment, she bit her lip. "I—I hadn't really thought of that."

"My building is really the safest place for you," he went on, "but there are all these deed restrictions, so I can't get you in there for longer than a week at a time—unless we're married."

"I see." Camille was right then. It was heroics on his part; he was trying to rescue the pathetic little orphan, and she was grateful, but that gratitude was like a stake in her heart. "C-couldn't I just go to a hotel somewhere?"

He was shaking his head. "I'd just have to stand guard there. Besides, it's cost prohibitive. Eibersen's not supposed to relocate to Alaska for two months."

Two months. Dear God, how would she endure two months as his wife, knowing that he didn't want the marriage? "It seems foolish to get married just for two months," she said softly.

"It's two months if he actually makes the move," Zach said through gritted teeth. "If he's as obsessive as I fear he is, he might not go at all."

Jillian tried very hard not to cry, but the tears finally defeated her. "I'm sorry," she whispered, "it's just that nothing seems to work out the way I want it to."

He nodded sharply and looked away. "Don't worry. I'll take care of everything. If Eibersen doesn't give up and leave town, I'll get rid of him somehow, I swear. Then we'll...file for a divorce. Or an annulment. Or...whatever." He suddenly laid his head back and sighed. "There's just one thing. We, um, we really ought to make out like this is the real thing, you know. If Eibersen suspects that it's a marriage in name only, no telling what he'll do. It complicates things because of my family, but I'll deal with them later. Right now, the important thing is just to get it done."

In name only. Jillian winced, pain slicing deep. "I—I'm not sure I can do it."

He looked at her then, surprisingly stern. "Oh, yes, you can. And you will." His voice softened, his eyes full of apology and regret. "You know I wouldn't insist if it wasn't the only solution. For now."

For now. Jillian wiped her eyes and nodded. Only for now.

* * *

On what should have been the happiest day of her life, Jillian stood before the justice of the peace in a simple, sleeveless white sheath with an overlay of chiffon that ended in points front and back, a halo of white rosebuds on her head. As befitted the situation, the Friday-morning ceremony was private and sparse. It wasn't real anyway, so it shouldn't have mattered, but Jillian couldn't quite make herself accept that. As much as she loved him—and she knew now that she did—she would have done just about anything to avoid this sham of a marriage. Her pride, and she was surprised to find that she had a good deal of it tucked away, rebelled at the idea of Zach sacrificing himself in a manner so obviously onerous to him.

But what else could she do? The thought of going back to Camille was even worse than the idea of being with Zach, and it wouldn't be fair to go back to the loft. She really had no other option, especially after the deli manager let her go. No doubt she had Camille to thank for that. But it didn't matter; nothing really did, except surviving the next two months as Zach's wife without losing her mind or doing something really stupid, like trying to make him love her. She knew, from bitter experience, the futility of that, and yet the temptation was great.

The past three days had been awful: sleeping in his bed while he made do with a cot in the living room; arranging a wedding no one wanted via telephone and quick, desultory shopping trips with a wary Zach; eating alone in the evenings while he vanished on one mission or another. She could only imagine what the coming weeks would be like, even with the larger apartment to which Zack had arranged to move.

Poor Zach. Poor honest, heroic Zach, who couldn't turn his back on a woman in distress, even if it meant marrying her and upending his whole life when he would obviously rather eat glass. She prayed that Janzen would give up and leave town immediately. Meanwhile, she had her exhibition to look forward to. Her art would keep her sane, especially as the new apartment was a two-bedroom unit so she could set up a studio in her room.

It would mean hanging a heavy plastic sheet over the doorway to keep dust out of the rest of the apartment and padding the walls with rubber foam sheets to contain the noise, but Zach didn't seem to mind. He seemed, in fact, to realize how important it was that she be able to work. She would be forever in Zach's debt for that alone—unless the sculpture sold right away, and she prayed that it would. Whatever happened, however, she would pay him back every penny he spent securing her safety. Somehow. First, though, she had to get through this "marriage."

Even if it was a sham, it seemed wrong to have a wedding without family or friends present, but Zach had insisted that it would be easier to explain to his family after the fact, and she couldn't bear to have her well-meaning chums around chirping congratulations when they weren't due. So it was just Jillian and Zach, the justice of the peace and two clerks from the JP's office, strangers all, really, for she did not know the Zachary Keller who stood next to her repeating meaningless vows in a monotone. The warm, frank, vastly entertaining man with whom she had fallen in love had been replaced by a nervous, irritable, withdrawn individual who couldn't even look her in the eye as he slipped the narrow, white-gold wedding band onto her finger. This man took his own ring from her and shoved it onto his hand impatiently, rather than waiting for her to work it over his broad knuckle. This man's lips were cool and stiff when he brushed them across hers at the conclusion of the brief service. He was brisk and terse afterward, driving straight back to the apartment to trade his suit and tie for faded jeans and a cream-colored T-shirt suitable for moving furniture and packing boxes.

Jillian changed into shorts and a camp shirt with the tails tied in a knot at her waist while Zach and a man provided by the apartment complex began dismantling his workout equipment for the move. When she emerged from the bedroom, Zach informed her that Denise was packing her tools and sculpture pieces, which would be delivered by the time they returned from visiting his family that evening.

"We're visiting your family this evening?" she asked, surprised.

He stopped what he was doing and regarded her solemnly. "Has to be done sometime. Might as well do it and get it over with. I told Brett we'd be at his place around seven, and he promised to call Dan and Mary and get them there."

"What did he say when you told him?" she asked self-consciously.

"I didn't. Just said I had someone I wanted them all to meet."

"And what about your parents?"

He looked down at the screwdriver in his hand and said, "I'll call them in Montana later. They're going to want us to come up there for a visit, which I don't think is a good idea. Any notion how to put them off?"

She shrugged, feeling lower than a hole in the ground. "The opening?"

He looked up at that. "Yeah, that might work. My wife the artist has an important show coming up and work to finish." He smiled, and for the first time, she felt her spirits lift. *My wife the artist. My wife.*

Just then the man helping to dismantle the workout equipment finished what he was doing and stood from a kneeling position. He looked directly at Jillian and asked, "What would you like me to do next, Mrs. Keller?"

The shock of her new name reverberated through her. Mrs. Keller. She opened her mouth, but the lump in her throat wouldn't let the words out.

Zach reached out to place a supportive hand on her shoulder, saying to the helper, "I think the plan is for you and me to move all this heavy stuff out while she packs up the kitchen. Isn't that right, Jillian?"

She managed a nod, and the two men began hoisting benches and rods onto a rolling dolly. Jillian got out of the way when they started pushing it toward the door, then took a deep breath and went into the kitchen. Some boxes were sitting on the counter. She began opening doors and drawers, removing the contents and deciding what to pack where. Working steadily and purposefully, she filled the boxes and went in search of more. Meanwhile, Zach and his helper came and went, loading and rolling out the items in the living room. By the time they were through, so was she. They stacked the boxes and rolled them down the hallway to the new apartment. She turned her attention to the bedroom.

By late afternoon the entire contents of the apartment had been moved. Then, to Jillian's surprise, deliverymen showed up with a new sofa to match the black leather armchair Zach already owned.

"I didn't know you were planning to do this," she said to Zach.

He shrugged. "If you don't like it we can always send it back."

"Whether I like it or not isn't the point. It's your couch. You're entitled to pick it out. I only meant that it wasn't necessary on my account."

"That's right," he said. "I bought it for me."

She stifled a spurt of disappointment, murmuring, "As long as you're clear on that."

He nodded. "I figured I could sleep on it until...well, I figured I could sleep on it."

She cocked her head. "What do you mean? Why should you sleep on the couch? I have my own bedroom now, and the cot will serve me just fine while I—"

"You can't sleep *and* work in there."

"Why ever not?"

He put his hands to his hips. "I saw the loft studio. You can't sleep with all that dust." She opened her mouth to explain that the fan she had rigged would suck up the majority of the stuff, but he held up a stifling finger. "You wouldn't be hanging plastic over the doorway if that contraption of yours took care of enough of it to make that room livable."

"But I won't let it get as bad as the loft. I'll clean regularly, every day if necessary, and—"

"And how much work will you get done that way?"

"Enough."

He shook his head stubbornly. "That room isn't big enough for your work table, materials, tools and a cot."

"I'll use a smaller table."

He rolled his eyes. "It won't work, Jillian. I've thought it all out."

"Then *I'll* sleep on the couch."

"We went through this when you first moved in," he said a little too loudly. "I like to work out late at night."

"Put the workout equipment in the bedroom."

"I like to watch TV while I work out," he said, almost shouting.

"Put the television in the bedroom," she said pleadingly.

Zach sighed and seemed to wilt before her eyes. It occurred to her that he must be as tired and confused as she was. "Why do you have to make this more difficult than it has to be?" he asked wearily.

Suddenly she wanted to run, to get as far away as possible from the reality of this unreal marriage, but where would she go? To Camille? Oh, yes, Camille would be happy to have her back. She could gloat forever over the sorry state of her pathetic little sister's pathetic mess of a life. Before Jillian quite knew what was happening, tears were rolling down her cheeks. Zach grimaced and threw a companionable arm around her shoulders.

"Here, now, what's this all about? Because I bought myself a comfy leather couch?"

She sniffed and wiped at her eyes with her fingertips, but the tears kept coming. "No," she choked out. "No."

"What then?"

She took a shuddering breath. "I don't know. It's my wedding day, I suppose. I don't know."

He let his arm slip away. "It's been a busy day. You'll feel better after a shower."

A shower. His family was expecting them tonight. "Yes. All right."

"We'll get a bite of dinner on the way," he said, moving away to begin putting his books back on the reconstructed shelves.

A bite of dinner. Their wedding supper. She mused silently that fast food would be sadly appropriate and headed for the bathroom.

Chapter Eight

Zach stood next to Jillian on the yard-square doorstep in front of his older brother Brett's modest brick veneer home, regretting the impulse that had brought him here. Why hadn't he just kept this nonsense to himself? It would all be over in a matter of months, if not weeks. His family never had to know that he had married. Did they?

Of course they did. What was he thinking? He couldn't keep a thing like this secret. It was just that he hated to lie to them, to let them think that this was a real marriage. The truth, however, brought its own complications, some of which he wasn't even willing to consider. So, he was taking the middle road, some truths, some lies. It seemed the only way.

The gentle pressure of a hand on his forearm reminded him that he was stalling. Inanely, he cleared his throat before lifting his hand to rap his knuckles on the door before reaching for the knob. The door opened before he could even turn the knob, and the small suntanned body of his six-year-old nephew appeared, a towel draped across his bare shoulders, dark hair glistening wet.

"Mo-o-om!" he bawled, "Uncle Zach's here—with a *girl!*"

The last he announced while disappearing down the darkened hallway.

Zach laughed, feeling instantly at home, and ushered Jillian into the entry hall with a hand at the small of her back. She pushed her glasses, still dark, up onto the top of her head. His sister-in-law, Sharon, in shorts and T-shirt, with his two-year-old niece parked on one hip, appeared, her red hair and freckled face a welcome beacon in the gloom. Her customary smile was in place, but her nut brown eyes widened comically when she saw for herself what her son had announced. She glanced back into the den.

"Brett Keller, you get up and get over here right now," she ordered good-naturedly. That done, she rushed down the hall to meet them. Going up on tiptoe, she smacked a welcome kiss on Zach's cheek, but her gaze remained targeted on Jillian, her eyes snapping with curiosity. Zach held back a teasing grin. He had no intention of enlightening anyone just yet.

"Are Danny and Mary here?"

"They're here," Brett said from the doorway. Advancing with that slow, loose-limbed stride of his, Brett looked Jillian up and down, his own curiosity held in polite check. He came to stand next to his wife, his forearm resting companionably on her shoulder. "They're out back watching the kids play in the sprinklers."

"Well, get 'em in here," Zach said, suddenly enjoying himself. "I only want to do this once."

Brett looked down at Sharon, one dark eyebrow crooking upward. "Okay," he said significantly, and strode away. Sharon's excited gaze seemed glued to Jillian.

"Won't you come in and have a seat?" she asked formally.

Jillian nodded and nervously reached up for her glasses, but Zach caught her hand midway and tugged her down the hall in Sharon's wake, winking at his niece, who grinned, stuck her finger in her mouth and laid her cheek against her mother's shoulder. When the little one shyly transferred her attention to the newcomer, Jillian smiled, receiving a tiny giggle as her reward.

Sharon's house was always comfortably rumpled like a made bed that someone had curled up on for a nap, and she never seemed to mind the scattering of children's things and the sprawl of Brett's ever-present sporting magazines. This evening, however, she set her daughter aside and hurried around the room, snatching up toys and neatening stacks, leaving Zach to usher Jillian to the couch. "Sorry everything's such a mess," Sharon said to no one in particular.

"Oh, the house is lovely," Jillian responded, and Zach gave her hand an appreciative squeeze, then exerted himself to coax his niece onto his lap and tickle her into her usual affectionate self. He was getting his head squeezed in an exuberant hug, much to Jillian's amusement, when the slap of bare feet on the kitchen floor alerted him that the invasion was under way. All three boys tumbled into the room, dancing and sashaying in their wet suits, showing off for company. Brett and Danny came next, ordering the kids upstairs to get changed, followed by a pregnant Mary, holding her sandy brown ponytail up off her neck with one hand and mopping her brow with a paper towel held in the other. Brett came over and plucked the baby off Zach, who kissed her feet as her daddy pulled her away. Brett turned her over his shoulder and held her in place with a big hand cupping her bottom.

"Okay, bro, we're all here. Let's do it."

Zach took Jillian's hand in his and propped his elbows on his knees. "Honey, I'd like you to meet my older brother, Brett, and his wife, Sharon. That's Shelby on Brett's shoulder there." Brett nodded acknowledgment, and Sharon smiled and gave a little wave. "This is my younger brother, Danny, and his wife, Mary." Danny made a little bow, his hands in the pockets of his chinos. Mary patted her rounded belly, smiling, and Zach amended his introduction. "Actually, that's Mary and Anthony Marshall, who ought to be able to make an entry on his own sometime next fall."

"Or before then if he starts walking as soon as his brother did," Mary added.

"Which one of those three is his brother?" Jillian asked, pointing toward the stairs up which the boys had disappeared moments earlier.

"The middle one," Mary said. "That's Jordan. He's five."

"And Andy is six, and Tim is four," Sharon put in.

"Okay," Zach said. "That's the lot, except for Mom and Dad, who are in Montana."

"Uh, not quite," Brett said, his voice deepening into that authoritative rumble that Zach knew so well. "I think you've missed one."

Zach looked at Jillian, working up his own courage as much as bolstering hers. She gave him a slight nod, and he rose to his feet, lifting her up with him. He slid an arm around her waist. "I want you to meet Jillian...Keller. My wife."

The announcement bomb whistled overhead, landed and exploded with a scream. Sharon literally leaped over the coffee table to be the first to get her hands on them, hugging and weeping all over them while Brett shoved the table out of the way and gave everyone room to gather around. When they emerged from hugs, laughter and exclamations some minutes later, the boys were back downstairs in various stages of dress, having been summoned by the commotion. Shelby had her fist in her mouth, trying to sort it all out as she perched on her father's shoulders. Zach sat down and pulled Jillian down next to him, his arm sliding up to drape about her shoulders in a motion that seemed wholly natural.

"When did you get married?" Mary demanded.

"This morning," Jillian replied softly.

"This morning!" Sharon exclaimed. "Zachary Keller, why didn't you let us know?"

"We didn't want to make a fuss," Zach said, crossing his legs.

"What I want to know is why you aren't off on your honeymoon?" Dan asked, for which Mary smacked him on the shoulder.

It was the moment Zach had dreaded, and to his distress, heat climbed up his throat. Jillian, bless her, came to his rescue.

"It was either a honeymoon or an apartment big enough for both of us," she said flippantly. "We spent the afternoon moving, actually, and now we only have to unpack it all and settle in."

"You gave up the bolt hole?" Brett teased.

"Well, we're still in the same building," Zach said, and the conversation was off, quickly becoming a girls and guys things, with the ladies talking all at once to one another and the guys breaking off to raid the refrigerator in the kitchen for cold drinks.

He got all the "sly devil" and "about time" cracks, and some stern advice concerning informing his parents. Zach cravenly asked Brett to break the news, promising he'd explain everything in detail later. The "details" encompassed an abbreviated version of the truth. Jillian worked in his building. They got close when he was brought in to help her sister, Camille Waltham—yes, that Camille Waltham—deal with a former fiancé. "Things just sort of snowballed," he admitted sheepishly.

"She's not a model, is she?" Dan asked carefully, sipping cold beer from the can.

"No, actually, she's a sculptor," Zach told him with an unexpected surge of pride. "She does some remarkable stuff, and she's got an exhibit coming up at this place in Deep Ellum called the Art Bar, I think."

"That's great!" Brett said. "Interesting, real interesting."

Zach smiled. This was going far more smoothly than he'd expected, almost too smoothly. He listened to the women's laughter in the other room and the screech and tumble of the kids, and it struck him that it was a perfect fit, he and Jillian, his brothers and their wives, a house full of kids. He'd always felt part of the family, of course, part of the gang, but somehow it was different tonight. If felt...complete. But how could that be? The marriage was a sham. This was all a desperate act on his and Jillian's part. How could it feel so right?

The women came into the kitchen, talking and laughing in a tight trio of instant friendship. Sharon stopped and slapped Zach lightly on the cheek. "Do you know what this jerk fed his bride on their wedding day?" she asked his brothers. "Barbecue sandwiches. Sandwiches!"

"That's more'n I fed you," Brett said, winking at Zach.

"At least you ordered a nice supper," Sharon said. "We just didn't get to it, is all."

Danny and Mary hooted. Brett elbowed Danny and made some

crack about his wife carrying proof that their seven-year honeymoon still wasn't over. "And he still hasn't fed me yet, either," Mary said to much laughter. "Maybe I ought to stop feed-
ing him."

It was all good-natured, if slightly colorful, banter, but Zach
couldn't help feeling that he ought to put a stop to it somehow.
He looked at Jillian, hoping she wasn't offended, only to find her
looking at him, a soft, wistful expression in her big blue eyes.
Was she wishing, maybe, that their marriage was real? She'd
made it plain from the beginning that she hadn't wanted to go
through with it, painfully so. Not that he could blame her. First
he'd refused to make love to her—a decision he knew was the
right one, given the circumstances—then he'd created a rupture
in her relationship with her sister, abandoned her to face it alone
and come to her aid only when it was almost too late. He couldn't
blame her for balking at his solution to her problems, but might
she change her mind if he showed her that he wanted more than
a temporary arrangement?

Good grief. What was he thinking? He didn't want to be married, either. Did he?

Suddenly he wasn't so sure. But was it because his family's
easy acceptance, their obvious approval, somehow colored his
feelings? Or did his feelings for Jillian go beyond liking, protectiveness and physical attraction? Was he falling in love with his
wife? He watched her pull her glasses down on her nose, their
lenses adjusted now to the indoor lighting, and very much feared
that he was.

"Let me hug your neck one more time, sugar," Sharon
crooned, wrapping her plump arms around Jillian's neck. "It's
so good to have you in the family."

Jillian gratefully returned the embrace, a bittersweet happiness
invading her. Zach's family had accepted her wholeheartedly,
without a single distrustful question or suspicious remark. If only
Zach could accept her so completely. He laid a hand on her
shoulder, and she pulled away from Sharon's parting hug, moving with him down the sidewalk toward the street.

"Y'all have a good weekend," Brett called. "We'll see you on Monday evening."

Jillian gave him a wave over her shoulder and let Zach hand her down into the car. He hurried around and got in behind the wheel as his brother and sister-in-law backed into the house and closed the door.

"That went well," he said, starting the engine.

"They're wonderful people."

"Yes, they are."

"You're so alike, you three brothers. Brett's a little heavier. Daniel's a little taller. But one glance and anyone would know you're brothers."

He hung an arm over the steering wheel thoughtfully. "You know, it's funny. When we were kids, we fought like bandits. Not that we hated one another or anything—just your normal sibling competition. Now, though, they're my very best friends."

Jillian sighed. "I used to think that one day Camille and I would be best friends, but somehow that never happened."

Zach sent her a glance that looked surprisingly guilty, but then he reached for the roof latch. "Let's put the top down."

She smiled. "And crank up the radio."

Laughing, they did just that. The radio was so loud that they turned some heads as they drove by on their way back to the apartment, so loud that it was impossible to talk over it. They let the valet park the car and went up to the apartment in silence, the tension growing tighter and thicker with every moment. It was their wedding night. Any normal couple would be looking forward to bed. As exhausted as she was, however, Jillian was dreading the moment she closed that door and lay down to sleep—alone.

She tried to tell herself that it was just like any other night, several of which she'd already spent in the same residence with Zach, but he hadn't been her husband then. Attraction hadn't matured into love. She thought of all he'd done to help her: putting up with Camille's high-handedness, repeatedly standing guard, letting her tag along while he searched for Janzen, defending her against Gerry's criticism, subtly building her confidence and, finally and most incredibly, marrying her to keep her safely away from Jan and give her a place to stay, lying to his own family in the process. Was it any wonder that she loved him? If only he could feel the same way about her. If only she weren't so pathetic and...*waifish.*

"Penny for your thoughts."

She looked up, surprised to find that they'd come to a halt in front of the apartment door. "Oh. Uh, actually my mind's a complete blank. I-I guess I'm just tired."

"It's been a busy day," he agreed, fishing in his pockets for the apartment key. "Darn," he said after a moment, "I knew I should have put that key on the ring right away." He dug around a moment longer. "I can't believe this. I don't have my key!"

Jillian opened her pocketbook. "I have mine." She looked through the meager contents of her bag, found the key on its little chain with its small red tag and handed it to Zach. Their fingers brushed as the key was transferred, a tiny electric spark snapping between them. Both jerked away. The key fell to the floor. Zach stepped back and bent to pick it up, then turned to fit it into the lock without ever looking up. In moments, they were in the apartment.

A half-dozen boxes were scattered around the room, their contents poking up and spilling over. Throw rugs lay rolled against the walls. Furniture warred with workout equipment for position. Still, it was a pretty apartment, much better than the dark cubby Zach had been living in. She silently vowed to make it as comfortable and homey as she could before she had to go.

A small dining area lay on the right of the entry, the kitchen behind it. Down a little farther on the left was a small nook with a closet for extra storage space, it's bi-fold doors standing open. The desk stood in front of it, partially blocking the small entry hall. An idea occurred to Jillian.

"You know, we could push the desk into the closet with the kneehole in the front, then we could just open the doors to sit at it. What do you think?"

"Hey, that's a good idea. An office in a closet, sort of. Might even be room for a small filing cabinet and a few shelves."

"Then you could put your workout equipment in the dining area, and if we moved the TV to that wall you could still watch it while you lift weights." She pointed to the space now occupied by a weight bench. Zachary nodded.

"Better and better." He paused. "Uh, you're sure, though? I thought you might want to get a dining set."

"Oh, not for two months," she said flippantly, wincing inwardly.

He looked away. "Right. No point in that."

"We can make do for meals at the bar between the kitchen and living room," she went on lightly, but she had forgotten something in her rush to appear unmoved by the prospect of ending her marriage. "That is, we could if we had bar stools."

"Good point. I'll see what I can do about that tomorrow."

"Don't go to any trouble," she said quickly. "It's only for—" Somehow she couldn't say it again. He did it for her.

"Two months. Yeah."

"We'll probably be eating off our knees in front of the television anyway," she said too brightly.

He nodded, mumbling, "That's what I usually do."

What he would do if his life was still his own, he meant. She bowed her head, biting back the urge to apologize for the mess she'd made of everything, his life included. What good were apologies when nothing could be changed by them?

"I'm, uh, bushed," she said, suddenly eager to escape. "I think I'll turn in."

"Yeah, me, too."

"Well, good night, then."

"Good night."

She headed across the living area toward the setback that opened onto both bedrooms and the single bath between them. As she moved toward the room on the right, the master, Zach said, "Hey, sleep as late as you want tomorrow."

"But we have so much to do yet," she argued, looking around them.

"We have the whole weekend to get this place into shape. One late morning won't hurt anything."

The whole weekend, alone together. "All right. Do you need anything before I go to sleep?"

"A pillow would be nice."

She walked into the room and took a pillow from the bed, his bed. She carried it back out to him and handed it over, careful not to touch. "Anything else?"

"No, I'll grab a sheet out of the box in the bathroom. Anything else I might need can wait until morning."

Nodding self-consciously, Jillian backed into the room and reluctantly closed the door, alone. On her wedding night.

Zach clutched the pillow to his middle with one hand, feeling empty and bereft. Life seemed damnably unfair at the moment. He was married to that woman, blast it all. He ought to be in there with her, undressing her slowly, indulging them both in the physical pleasures about which his brothers and their wives joked so easily. So what if it was only temporary? He deserved something for all the trouble he was going to, didn't he?

The resentful thought soured even as he justified it with a litany of the ways his life had changed since he'd met Jillian Waltham. Jillian Waltham *Keller*. A sudden fierce possessiveness pushed aside all else. She was his wife. His wife. The funny thing was that it didn't seem strange at all. His family had certainly found no reason to question it, despite the fact that the marriage was totally unexpected. As a matter of fact, they had liked her, very much.

He carried the pillow to the couch and dropped it there before going to open the vertical blinds on the large bank of windows set in the outside wall. This apartment had a lovely view, not the downtown vista of lit skyscrapers found on the opposite side of the building, but the parklike serpentine of Turtle Creek and the twinkling, undulating sweep of neighborhoods and street lamps that glowed amber in the hot black night. Zach sat down on the couch and tugged off his boots, letting them lie where they fell. It was a comfortable piece of furniture, the leather butter soft and silky, the cushions deep and springy, a great improvement on the stiff cot on which he'd been tossing and turning these past nights, but he knew he wasn't going to sleep again tonight. It was his wedding night, and the woman with whom he wanted to share it lay alone behind a closed door. Might she welcome him if he went to her? She had once before.

With a shake of his head, he reminded himself that he had humiliated her by his rejection, however unintentional, and then left her to deal with the aftermath on her own, even knowing that she was in danger from an obsessive suitor. She had made her feelings clear on this notion of marriage. He couldn't blame her. She'd just found a freedom of sorts from her sister's egotistical tyranny, and now, through sheer necessity, was married to the man who had forced the issue by his actions, endangering her in the process. No, she would be insane to welcome him now. With a sigh of resignation, he realized that he was living a homily. He had made his bed, and now he had to sleep in it. Alone.

Jillian dozed fitfully, her mind whirling with the events of the past, some she had all but forgotten. For a brief moment, she was a little girl playing on the deck with her parents sipping cold drinks beside her, sunning themselves on chaise lounges and murmuring to each another about the upcoming week. Her third-grade teacher handed her a blue ribbon she'd won on a water-color painting. She posed for pictures at a birthday party, happy and tired.

Other memories came. Camille, at twelve, informed her haughtily that her beloved mother was a home breaker. Her father explained that he had been unhappily married to Gerry when he'd fallen in love with her own mother, who wept silent tears at the telling. Jillian half remembered, half dreamed Gerry declaring that her parents should pay for what they had done to her. She dreamed reluctantly of the policeman who had come to her friend Meredith's house to inform her that her parents were lost at sea in the Gulf of Mexico. They would not be returning from their weekend jaunt. She heard Meredith's mother telling her that she could stay with them just as long as she needed to, and she remembered feeling sick and knowing that it wasn't so. Meri had three sisters and two brothers residing in their comfortable middle-class home.

Camille came for her, and Jillian remembered her relief and gratitude. She hadn't believed it would happen. Gerry, stiff-lipped and disapproving, stood aside as Gerry's current husband and Jillian wagged her packed baggage into the house. She remembered that same man, less than a year later, shouting at Gerry that her bitterness ruined everything around her as he stormed from the house. She remembered, too, that Gerry had blamed Jillian's father even for that, though he was dead and gone. Worst of all, she remembered Camille's silent agreement.

Other slights came to her, criticisms on everything from her attitude to her clothing, disparaging remarks about her looks and her interests, mockings of her friends. She remembered good things, too: she and Camille laughing together over something silly; Camille whispering that they were sisters and would always be together; infrequent compliments on the smallest things, some supper dish, the whiteness of a freshly laundered pair of socks, a comment on a report card. She remembered celebrating Camille's achievements, Gerry's third wedding and the relief of having her move out of the house. In those relatively peaceful years following, Jillian had tagged along to important parties, double-dated as a stand-in for one of Camille's friends who had canceled at the last minute, had her first boyfriend, a shy chemistry geek whose idea of a date was eating lunch together in the school cafeteria.

Jillian mourned the slow death of Gerry's late husband, who had given Gerry a measure of happiness that had controlled her resentment, and felt the sting of casual breakups and promised calls that never came, unrequited crushes and shameful longings. But she relished other memories, the enthusiastic encouragement of certain teachers, making new friends in college, developing new interests, honing her talent. She remembered moving to the new house Camille bought in North Dallas, Gerry joining them again, the wavering hope that they could fashion a true family of sorts.

In the nether world of semiconsciousness, Jillian relived the

surge of triumph and achievement that came with insight into her
own creativity, laughter with her friends, the dawning certainty
of Denise's quirky friendship, the fun of Worly's infamous jam
sessions. She felt herself narrowing and expanding at the same
time, trying to fit the ever more confining mold fashioned for her
by Camille, breaking free of that cocoon of neediness when away
from her. Then the real nightmares came.

Visions of her parents tossing lifelessly in a rough, black sea
broke her heart. Gerry, on a drunken rampage after her second
divorce, scared and embarrassed her. Camille screamed at her
that she couldn't do anything right and threw a blue dress with
a scorch mark on it in her face. And Janzen. Smiles and winks
were followed by rages and pleading apologies. Jillian covered
her ears to block out screaming matches between him and Camille. She shrugged away unwanted touches, listened uneasily to
offensive teasing, pretended to misinterpret loaded looks and
guiltily ignored Gerry's innuendos. She suffered Camille's accusing looks and disparaging denials, and then she awoke, startled, to the darkness of her own bedroom and Janzen's alcohol-
heated breath and fumbling hands. Locked doorknobs rattled,
Janzen's slurred voice pleading, promising. Camille screamed
and wailed while Gerry accused and guilt swamped her. The
telephone rang endlessly. Tires screeched and metal crunched.
Camille hissed for her to keep quiet. Shattering glass showered
her face. A dark, menacing presence knocked her to the floor.
Pain blinded her, and in the same moment she was alone in her
room in the dark. No, not alone. Someone else was there. She
screamed. Zach! Where was Zach?

Suddenly she was in his arms, safe and trembling, as he murmured words of comfort and apology. Gradually she realized that
daylight had chased back the shadows of night. The pounding of
her heart slowed and then sped up again as she became aware
of where she was and why. This was not her bedroom but Zach's,
and it was the morning after her wedding.

"I'm sorry," Zach was saying. "I didn't mean to frighten you.
I just came in to get some clean clothes."

Her sham wedding. A wedding night spent alone. Lies and

desperate schemes. Friendly people easily fooled. A husband who didn't love her. Nowhere else to go. Temporary, a temporary life to which she must not become accustomed. Jillian eased out of his embrace and settled back onto the pillow, a hand going to her head where the ache of exhaustion and unhappiness thudded dully. "I was dreaming."

"Nothing pleasant, apparently."

She sighed, figuring it was better not to answer. "What time is it?"

"Early. I was just about to go out for coffee and some breakfast. I'll bring something for you."

"Oh, no, that's not necessary. I'll find something here."

"I meant that I was going to bring something back for the both of us to have together."

She smiled at that, then reminded herself that it was foolish to do so. Zach was always thoughtful with everyone. It meant nothing, really. She pushed up on one elbow. "You don't have to do that. I'll fix something. I know just where the coffeepot is."

He pushed her back down with a gentle hand on her shoulder. "Nothing doing. You can play housewife later if you've a mind to. Right now I think you could use a little more sleep."

She was tired. She hadn't exactly rested last night, and she couldn't help wondering if it had been the same for him. "How about you?" she asked casually. "Did you sleep well?"

"Like a baby." He smiled and got up off the side of the bed, pulling down the hem of his T-shirt, which had been bunched up around his chest. She guessed that he'd been pulling it on when she'd startled awake and tried to fix her thoughts on that rather than her shameful disappointment that he had not shared the difficulties of the long night with her.

"I won't be long," he said, grabbing a pair of socks from a box on top of the dresser. "If you're asleep when I get back, I'll stash your food in the oven. Okay?"

"Fine."

He started for the door, then turned back and snagged a key identical to the one in her purse off the dresser, then held it up with a smile to show her that he'd remembered it this time. She rolled onto her side as he left the room, and stared unseeingly at the jumble of items crammed into the corner below the window. The tears caught her unaware, flooding her eyes and spilling onto her cheeks with a wrenching sob. She turned her face into the pillow and wept for what was not and would never be.

Zach let himself out of the apartment and moved listlessly down the hallway toward the elevator. He had begun to wonder if the night would ever end, when the first rays of the sun finally lightened the world to a dull gray. Only then had he actually slept, sheer relief aiding exhaustion to overpower his beleaguered mind, but that slumber had been brief and unsatisfactory, yielding only an hour or so later to the hungry rumblings of his belly and the renewed plague of his thoughts. He had to get out of the apartment, away from the woman sleeping alone in his bed, his reluctant wife. He'd showered and shaved, moving quietly but quickly, only to find that the steam had done nothing to smooth the wrinkles in his shirt. That was when he'd decided to slip into the bedroom and find something more presentable.

At first she'd seemed to be sleeping peacefully. He'd foolishly stopped to watch her. As before, she lay on her side, one hand tucked beneath her cheek. Her long, pale eyelashes were as fine as cobwebbing, her mouth a perfect pink bow, her chin a delicate point. Even with her caramel hair sticking out at odd angles, she was beautiful, and he marveled that he hadn't seen it sooner, hadn't recognized the delicacy and utter uniqueness of her behind that dowdy uniform and ugly glasses when she had greeted him from behind the deli counter. But what use were regrets of that fashion? He couldn't go back now to smile at her, to flirt a little and then a little more. It was too late to engineer friendly chats and even friendlier, longer, talks, to hint interest and finally to ask for a proper date. Too late for what had never been.

It was when he had turned away to find and pull on a T-shirt that she had cried out, a hoarse, startled sound that had told him immediately of her fear and shock. Reflexively, he'd turned and caught her up, wanting nothing more than to protect her from the very fear he'd unintentionally instigated, and she had clung to him as naturally as before—before he'd rejected her, abandoned her. Before he'd married her. But then she'd pulled away, whereas before she'd ultimately offered herself, not just her body but her whole self, and he'd known it even then. God, what a fool he was, what a coward, to have turned down all that she had offered. Not that he now believed he should have made love to her that night. On the contrary, he knew without any doubt that the one noble thing he'd done, the one thing he'd gotten right, was not taking her virginity that night. What he should have taken, however, was everything else she'd offered, her heart, her love, her unique and bewitching self. Had he done so, he wouldn't have spent his wedding night alone and tortured. He would be with her now, loving her with his body and his soul, pleasantly exhausted from the sheer joy of it, instead of stumbling tired from a long night of recrimination and regret.

Zachary Keller, smarter than the system, braver than the cops with their badges and backup, defender of women and the abused, hero to the persecuted. Blithering idiot. Clumsy fool. A necessary but unwanted husband who was realizing too late that he was hopelessly in love with his wife.

Chapter Nine

They spent the day moving around the furniture they'd moved in the day before until both were satisfied. Lunch consisted of cold sandwiches and iced tea. Jillian built the sandwiches, using her vast experience, and Zach made the tea with instant powder and so much sugar Jillian had to "cut" hers with lemon juice. As the day wore on, the unacknowledged tension between them eased, so that they began to gently tease each other. The teasing brought such relief that they began to clown around. By late afternoon Jillian was as wearied from laughter as physical exertion. Zach seemed to be dragging, too. When he suggested that it was time to call a halt for the day, Jillian didn't argue. Collapsing into opposite corners of the sofa, their feet and lower legs entangling, they groaned as one, heads falling back, arms flung out, and settled in to let exhausted muscles rest.

"Do you know," Jillian said after a moment, "we haven't completely unpacked a single box yet?"

Zach moaned and sat up a little straighter, disentangling their feet by crossing one ankle over the other knee and shifting slightly to one side. "Maybe it would be easier to just drop it all down the garbage chute."

Jillian felt the sharp sting of guilt. Sitting up straight and leaning forward earnestly, she said, "I'm sorry, Zach. I'm so very sorry."

"For what?" he asked, sounding genuinely puzzled.

"For upsetting your whole life with my personal problems. I never meant for any of this to happen, you know. That first day when I came into your office, I was genuinely worried that Janzen was going to hurt my sister, but I messed up everything by not telling you the truth about their breakup. And now look at you."

"Yeah, just look at me," he said dryly, turning glances all around him. "I'm finally out of that dark hole and into the nifty apartment that I promised myself when I first moved in here."

"If that's really how you feel, then why didn't you make the move earlier?"

He shrugged. "You know how it is. You get into a rut, work all the time, let your private life go to hell. You figure no one's ever going to see this rat hole but you, so why go to all the trouble to box everything up and move?"

She threw her arms out in a deprecating gesture. "And now you're just thrilled, I suppose."

He leaned forward, forearms balanced on his knees. "Listen. I chose this building for its security after my last place was ransacked by a jealous husband who thought I was hiding his wife. I'd helped her move to a shelter to get away from him, but he thought all wives were supposed to do double duty as punching bags and just couldn't figure that a few black eyes and broken ribs would drive her off, so it had to be another man luring her away."

"Sounds like Camille," Jillian commented wryly.

Both of Zach's eyebrows shot up. "You're exactly right. Anyway, I realized it wasn't likely to be the only time some bad guy came looking for me, so I did a little research and came up with this place. They had one apartment available at the time—aside from the penthouse, that is. The place was so bleak my brother started calling it the bolt hole, and I wasn't exactly thrilled to be calling it home at first, but then, like I said, you get used to things and you figure it's not worth bothering about.''

"And then you have your hand forced..." Jillian reflected leadingly.

He sat back, shaking his head. "You like being the whipping boy, don't you?''

Before she could answer that, his cell phone rang. He snatched it off his belt, pulled out the antenna and answered. "Keller.'' After a moment he sighed and said, "Okay. Call Withers and tell him I'm on my way.'' He shut off the phone and clipped it onto his belt again. Standing, he said to Jillian, "I've got to go. One of my subcontractors, Kent, is having car trouble, and it's time for a shift change. Normally, it wouldn't be a problem, but apparently the guy I have to take over for has a hot date waiting for him. I shouldn't be longer than a few hours.''

"Is it Janzen?'' she asked worriedly.

"No. It's another case. Gabler and Padgett are on Eibersen. Don't worry. We've got him covered. He can't get to you here.''

"I'm not worried about me,'' she told him.

Zach reached out a hand to smooth her hair, smiling softly. "Surely you aren't worried about me.''

Her throat suddenly constricted. Clearing it nervously, she said, "Your work is dangerous. You told me so yourself.''

He nodded. "Which is why I take every precaution. This isn't a case of violence, however. This is a guy trying to skip out on paying his child support by claiming he's injured and can't work. So far we've filmed him and his 'bad back' washing and waxing his truck, trimming his trees and mowing his yard. Now we're just trying to make sure he doesn't skip town before the case comes to a hearing.''

"I see.''

"Good. I've really got to go now. I'll call if I'm going to be late. Why don't you order in pizza or something for dinner?''

She wrinkled her nose, thinking that she'd had her fill of pizza for a long while during her stay with Denise and Worly. "Chinese, maybe.''

He nodded, and she got up and followed him to the door. "I'll leave some money at the desk,'' he was saying. "You won't even have to go down. One of the security guards will bring it up."

"Great," she answered, trying to sound enthusiastic and failing miserably.

He stopped in the doorway to reassure her once more. "I'll be back before you know it. Save me some cashew shrimp."

"Right. Cashew shrimp."

Smiling, he bent forward slightly, and for just a moment she thought he was going to kiss her goodbye. Instinctively, she turned up her mouth, only to feel his lips against her forehead. She closed her eyes so he wouldn't see her disappointment and an instant later heard him move away. Shutting the door, she leaned her back against it and tried to regain her equilibrium. It struck her then that the only thing worse than spending the day alone with Zach was spending the evening alone without him.

Zach backed the truck into its space and killed the engine. He was tired and hot but felt an unaccustomed enthusiasm at the same time. It really was different, coming home to a bright, spacious apartment instead of a dark, cave-like cubby hole. He hopped out of the truck and strode through the parking garage to the lobby, stepping into mercifully cool air. The guard at the desk looked up from his monitor and waved.

"Hello, Mr. Keller. Still hot out there?"

"You know it."

"Worse summer since '80, they're saying."

"I believe 'em."

He moved behind the desk and headed toward the elevators. "My wife send out for dinner?"

"Yes, sir. I took it up myself on my break. Nice woman, Mrs. Keller. Gave me a tip."

Zach chuckled. "Good for her." The elevator door opened, and he stepped inside. Somewhere between the second floor and the third, it struck him how easily he'd used and accepted those words. My wife. Mrs. Keller. Who was he kidding, trying to tell himself that it was the new apartment he was eager to get home to? The apartment meant nothing without someone with whom to share it, which was why he hadn't bothered to move before now, but it wasn't just anyone he was eager to get home to. It was Jillian he wanted to see, even though being with her was like having an ache that he couldn't quite identify, let alone ease.

The elevator slowed and stopped. He stepped off and walked down the hallway, taking out his keys. Quickly, he let himself into the apartment. The quiet told him that Jillian had retired early. It was only about half past eight, but she'd worked hard all day, and he doubted that she'd rested well the night before, given the way she'd awakened that morning. She deserved a good rest, but he had to fight back disappointment as he walked into the kitchen and flipped on the indirect lighting.

The kitchen was neat and immaculate, the boxes gone, the counter scrubbed. Apparently she'd been busy in the hours he'd been away. He opened the refrigerator, looking for the leftovers he'd counted on for dinner. To his surprise, he found three un-opened cardboard containers on the shelf, all full. Why hadn't she eaten? Puzzled, he walked into the living room, wondering if he ought to knock on the bedroom door. It was then that he saw her. She'd made him a bed on the couch, bottom sheet neatly tucked in, top sheet folded across one arm of the couch, and then she'd apparently lain down to wait for him—and waited still, one hand tucked under her cheek, knees drawn up.

She was wearing her sleep shirt, that long, blousy T-shirt that looked more like a dress than a nightgown. Unfortunately, it wasn't quite long enough. With her legs curled up like that, her neat bottom was left exposed, save for a patch of pale-pink nylon pantie that made his heart race almost painfully. He cleared his throat, hoping that was all it would take to awaken her. She merely sighed and snuggled more deeply into the cushions, her arm settling into the indentation of her waist and drawing the skirt even higher. Zach gulped, his hand trembling as he thought about cupping that sleek, rounded cheek. From there, he could slide his fingers down into the cleft between her thighs and... Blood surged into his groin, and he shook his head, dislodging the dangerous imaginings. Bending, he reached forward and quickly tugged down her shirt, saying her name at the same time. "Jillian."

She jerked slightly, then rolled backward and opened her eyes, smiling up at him. "You're home."

He had to look away from her, remembering all too well how she felt in his arms, her pliant skin warm and silky, her gentle curves so utterly female. "You, um, didn't eat."

She sat up, pushing hair out of her eyes. "I was waiting for you."

"You didn't need to do that," he said more brusquely than he'd intended.

"I wanted to."

"Well then, you must be as hungry as I am."

She got up and started toward the kitchen. "I'll get everything ready. You must want to wash up."

"Right." Washing up was no more what he wanted at the moment than Chinese food, but those things would just have to do.

He made quick work of the washing up, noticing as he did so that she'd been busy in the bathroom, too. No wonder she was so tired. When he reemerged into the living area, he saw that she had laid out plates and napkins on the bar, while the microwave hummed. The timer dinged as he drew near, and she turned away to transfer the now steaming cardboard containers to the countertop. "You want a fork or chopsticks?" she asked, opening a drawer and taking out each.

"Neither. Give me a soupspoon. I'm too hungry to eat dainty."

"Spoons it is." She laid out five, one for each of them and three to serve the steamed rice, cashew shrimp and sweet-and-sour chicken.

"You've been busy," he said, filling his plate while she filled her own.

She shrugged. "I just put the kitchen to rights. Hope you don't mind."

"Why would I mind?"

"Well, it is your place."

He dropped the spoon into the carton and looked at her. "As long as you're here, this is *our* place. Besides, I don't know anything about organizing a kitchen."

"I noticed that when I packed the other one," she said wryly.

He chuckled. "I didn't figure it mattered. Wasn't much to organize."

"I noticed that, too."

They carried their plates into the living room and sat down on the sofa. He pulled up his feet and propped one elbow on the arm of the couch, his plate balanced on his palm. "We'll do some shopping," he said, "pick up anything you think we need."

"We can make do as we are," she said unconcernedly, and began to eat.

He shoveled down the first plate and went back for more. When he returned to the couch, she asked conversationally, "How did your business go?"

"Fine. Kent's problem was just a dead battery, easily taken care of. As far as the case goes, our bird doesn't seem to be preparing to fly the coop anytime soon. I don't think he even knows he's been found out. Hearing is set for Tuesday, so we're on short time."

"Good work."

"I work with good people."

She spooned up a small bite of battered chicken in bright orange-pink sauce, chewed and swallowed. "How does that happen exactly—this subcontracting stuff?"

He explained as he ate. "I take bids every quarter from a number of operatives. They submit written figures, how much they expect per hour for what activity, how many hours they're willing to work overall, when they're available. I look at how much training and experience they have, check their references, if necessary, and make the best 'buys' I can. For that quarter, I agree to call on those subcontractors whose bids I accept. Over the years I've learned which operatives I work best with, which I can count on most, but I'm always open to new talent."

"Sounds complicated," she said, bending forward to place her empty plate on the floor.

He dug around in his rice, looking for cashews. "Yeah, sometimes it's more trouble than just hiring on a staff, withholding all the taxes and providing the required benefits, but I keep at it. One of these days, though, I'm going to expand in that direction and settle into running the show rather than covering the street."

"Wouldn't that be safer than the way you're doing it now?"

He nodded. "I suppose so, yeah."

"But you just can't give up working the street, can you?" she asked quietly.

He kept his gaze trained on his plate, though his hunger was fully sated now. "It's not that. Just never had a reason to give it up." He measured what he was going to say next, aware that his heart was beating harder than normal. "I always thought I'd give it up once I got married."

"*Really* married, you mean," she said almost offhandedly.

Irritation flashed through him, irritation combined with a dark disappointment. He shot up off the couch, his spoon clanking against his plate. "You say that like we're *not* really married! How much more really married do you think you can get?"

"I didn't mean it that way," she replied with maddening calm. "I know how big a sacrifice you've made."

"Whose talking about sacrifice?" he exclaimed. "I'm just saying that we are *really* married."

"I know, but it's only temporary."

He wanted to lash out at her for that, but how could he when she was absolutely right? "Still," he muttered, "we are *really* married."

"I know."

"Fine." Bending, he swept up her plate, then carried it to the kitchen with his own. He dumped the contents into the side of the sink with the garbage disposal, rinsed the plates and put them into the dishwasher, then closed the food containers and stashed the leftovers in the refrigerator. When he returned to the living room, Jillian was sitting in the corner with her legs folded, staring out the window thoughtfully. He sat down and tried for a light, conversational tone.

"So, what else did you do while I was gone?"

She glanced at him, then away again. "I took a bubble bath, a nice, long, relaxing soak."

He wished he hadn't asked. Just the thought of her lolling there in the tub, naked and surrounded by hot water and frothy bubbles, tied him in knots. He bounced up off the couch again, saying, "Speaking of baths, I really need a shower."

"Zach, wait," she said, unfolding her long legs and coming after him. He stopped in his tracks and turned back to her, surprised to find her so close. She backed up, right into the end of the couch, the rolled arm hitting her at the tops of her thighs. She balanced herself and inched forward again. "I, um, I didn't mean to upset you."

He shook his head, his hands at his waist. "I'm not upset."

"Yes, you are. The question is, why?"

He prepared to bluff his way through, but did he really want to? He knew what he wanted, and maybe, just maybe, she wanted the same thing. Shouldn't he at least find out? He took a single step toward her. "I just don't like the idea that you don't seem to think of yourself as being really married to me."

"I think of myself as being really married to you," she said. "I just don't want you to think that I expect more of you than you're willing to give."

"No?" He stepped closer still.

"I think you've gone way above and beyond the call of duty or friendship for me already. In fact, I think you're my hero."

"That's a lot of thinking," he said softly, and she smiled. "Want to know what I think?"

"Why not."

He lifted a hand and slid it into her hair at the back of her head. "I think you're beautiful," he whispered, bending his head to bring his mouth next to hers, that sweet, pink Cupid's bow that had yielded so sweetly before. Her eyes were huge, as blue as a morning sky. When she closed them, her lids shuttering down, he felt the exhilaration of triumph, but the instant his mouth met hers, desire obliterated all else. Cupping the back of her head, he slid his lips against hers. Lifting her arms around his neck, she moaned softly, and he filled her with his tongue, tasting and teasing, plunging and retreating to plunge again, over and over, deeper and deeper, until suddenly they were toppling over the arm of the couch, legs tangling, bodies bumping.

"Zach," she gasped, scrambling backward on her elbows, legs wrapping around him. He followed her, seeking her mouth again, reveling in the feel of her body beneath his, tussling for space on the couch. One hand found the silky fabric of her panties and slid down to cup her bottom, lifting and pressing her against the throbbing hardness in his groin as his booted feet fought the arm of the couch. She grabbed his head with both hands and pulled. At that moment, he got one foot in place and pushed, driving his body against her. He found her mouth and plunged his tongue inside, rocking his hips into the vee of her thighs. She hooked her heels into the backs of his knees and thrust upward. He thought he'd explode.

When she tugged feverishly at his T-shirt, he yanked it off, pulling it up between them and breaking the kiss long enough to get his head free. The arms came next, then he flung the garment over the back of the couch, even as he pressed her down once more, his mouth seizing hers. He moved against her, breath coming in gasps as he kissed her again and again, finally stabbing his tongue inside as she surged upward, grinding against him until the need to be inside her was as much pain as desire. He slid one hand between them, fumbling with his fly. She jerked and clawed at him as his knuckles brushed against her panties. The zipper finally went down, and he raised up onto his knees, reaching for the tiny elastic waistband of her panties. It was then that she suddenly scrambled backward, up into the corner of the couch. He froze.

"What?"

Didn't she want him? Had he read it all wrong?

Her breasts heaved against the fabric of her gown. "W-we could accidentally make a b-baby!"

A baby. He reeled mentally, trying to fully grasp the reality of the situation. Was she saying she didn't want him or that she didn't want a baby? Or was it both?

"We shouldn't," she gasped, drawing her legs up. "It isn't right if we're only going to be together two months."

Two months. She was telling him that whatever happened, she wouldn't be staying longer than the necessary two months. She was his wife for two months only. Zach sat back on his heels, feeling as though she'd opened his chest and ripped his heart out. If only it were that easy! He blinked and slowly shifted his legs out from beneath him so that he sat on the couch. Leaning forward, he propped his elbows on his knees and buried his face in his hands.

"Zach," she whispered, her fingertips brushing his shoulder.

He jerked away. If she touched him now, he wouldn't be responsible for what happened next.

"Oh, Zach," she sighed, moving closer. Suddenly he knew he had to get out of there before he did something he'd regret.

Rising to his feet, he turned away, muttering breathlessly, "I'm going to take a shower—a cold shower."

"Zach," she said again, but he didn't turn back this time, didn't even pause until he'd closed the bathroom door between them.

He turned on the tap, yanked off his boots and shoved down his jeans and briefs, then stepped out of them. Stripping off his socks, he got into the shower and let the cold water pour over his head and shoulders until it gradually warmed. She wanted him, but not enough to stay, not enough to risk a baby. Now he knew. Now he knew. And now he wished he didn't.

Sunday was devoted to unpacking boxes and organizing the apartment. Both Jillian and Zach slept late, ate little and spoke only as necessary. The easy camaraderie of the day before was gone, driven out by unsated passion and private hurts. Jillian felt on the verge of tears all day, and it was almost with relief that she greeted the telltale ringing of Zach's cell phone—until she realized the call had to do with Janzen. She listened with bated breath to the one-sided conversation until Zach hung up the phone.

"What's happened?"

Zach sighed and leaned a shoulder against the wall. "Padgett was watching Eibersen last night. Eibersen got drunk in his motel room and tried to get in his car and drive off but couldn't get the door unlocked, so he struck out on foot. Apparently he was so drunk that Padgett was worried he'd fall into the street and get hit by a car, so eventually Padgett pulled over and offered him a ride. Eibersen asked to go to Camille's house, said he had to find out where you are."

"Dear God," Jillian whispered. Was Camille still in danger?

Zach went on. "Seems he went to the deli last week and was told you weren't working there anymore, so he figured to make Camille tell him where he could find you. According to Padgett, Eibersen was babbling about Camille making you pretend you didn't want him to keep him away from you and how he wouldn't believe it because the two of you are meant to be together. He kept saying that she had brainwashed you, that he had to show you that you belong with him instead of her hand-picked stooge, meaning me, I suppose."

Jillian sighed and put a shaking hand to her head. "This would be funny if it wasn't so frightening."

"Yeah, like Camille wants us together," Zach commented wryly.

"Or like you would be anyone's *stooge*," she said. "What did Padgett do?"

The corner of Zach's mouth lifted in a semismile. "He bought Eibersen a few more drinks. Eibersen finally passed out, and Padgett took him back to the motel and put him to bed."

Jillian closed her eyes in relief. "That's good. He didn't get to Camille then."

"It's not that good," Zach said. "Eibersen knows Padgett now, which means I've got to find someone else to cover him."

Jillian bit her lip. "This thing has gotten so complicated. Why can't he just leave us alone?"

Zach folded his arms, inclining his head. "According to Dr.

Shorter, this behavior is usually compulsive. Mix in the alcohol, and you've got a person pretty much out of control."

Jillian lifted worried eyes to unreadable ones. "What's going to happen, Zach?"

For a long moment he didn't answer, but then he shook his head. "I don't know. I just don't know." With that he turned and walked away.

Jillian spent Monday setting up her studio. Zach went into the office as usual, called twice to see if she needed anything and came home late, apparently expecting her to be ready to go to his brother's for dinner as planned. Jillian had showered and was in a confusing panic, trying to decide what to wear, when he showed up at the bedroom door.

"You aren't ready?"

She ignored the question on the grounds that the answer was all too obvious. "Zach, thank goodness! Tell me what to wear tonight!"

Eyebrows aloft, he walked over to the bed and looked down at the variety of dresses and dressy slacks laid out there; then, hands on hips, he walked over to the closet and went through her things. In short order he extracted a pair of dark jeans and a little lace top that wrapped and buttoned at the waist. "Something go under this?" he asked, holding up the lace top.

"A kind of camisole," she said, rushing to a dresser drawer.

"Okay, then. Wear this." He handed over the jeans and cream-colored top.

"Are you sure?"

"Yep."

"What about shoes?" she asked, running to the closet and grabbing a pair of flats and a pair of sandals, both made of cream leather.

He pointed at the sandals. "Those."

He sounded so sure of his choices. "Okay, okay. What do you think about a belt?" She grabbed the hanger with all her belts on it out of the closet. He looked them over and picked a skinny gold chain with a pearl drop on one end.

She threw the stuff on the bed and yanked the towel off her wet head. Her hand went to the belt of her bathrobe, as she kicked off her house shoes. "Well, what are you waiting for?" she asked, realizing that he was just standing there grinning at her.

"Just enjoying this classic married moment," he said, chuckling.

She smiled as he left the room, closing the door carefully behind him. He was right. It was just the sort of thing that husbands and wives went through all the time, and it felt good, too good.

When she came out of the room a few minutes later, her hair fluffed dry and spritzed into face-framing spikes, glasses perched protectively on the bridge of her nose. Zach shook his head, and her spirits plummeted. "What? What's wrong?"

Zach plucked the glasses off her nose and tossed them onto the bar. "You don't need those things, and we both know it. Now let me look at you." He caught her hands and lifted her arms to shoulder height, his gaze sweeping her. After a moment, he smiled and complimented them both, saying, "I do good work. Maybe I ought to branch out, go into fashion consulting. You look delicious."

She felt delicious with his green eyes all but eating her where she stood. "Thanks. You're sure it's okay?"

"You questioning my taste?" he asked with mock severity.

She laughed. "Not at all."

"Good. Let's get moving. We're already a few minutes late."

She cast a last look at the discarded glasses and let him shepherd her to the door. They hurried down to find the convertible waiting for them, the air conditioner cooling at full blast. Jillian plucked at her hair with her fingertips, smoothing it against her nape. It was in need of a trim, but she hadn't wanted to bother with it, all things considered. She couldn't wait for Janzen to leave town before she next visited the hairstylist, but since she dared not go out by herself, she would have to have an escort, which seemed like a prodigious amount of bother for a little haircut.

"It looks great," Zach said, seeming to read her mind, and she dropped her hand to her lap, smiling.

They pulled up in front of Brett's house and parked at the curb. "I like your brother and sister-in-law a great deal," Jillian said, "but I'm feeling really guilty about this."

Zach sighed. "I know. It doesn't seem fair, does it?"

"Breaking the news was one thing," Jillian added, "but socializing like we're one big happy family is another. On top of that, I'm afraid I'll say or do something to give us away."

"I'll stay close," he assured her. "It'll be okay."

Jillian shot him a doubtful look. "You know, on Friday when we were here and they invited us for dinner tonight, it didn't seem like such a big deal, but suddenly this afternoon I realized they think we're in love, that we've been sleeping together all weekend. They probably think we've been having wild, romantic sex all this time!"

"Just shows how much they know," he muttered, yanking open the car door. "It'll be all right," he said, walking around the car as she let herself out on her side. "And we won't accept any more invitations. We can say you're trying to get ready for your opening."

Jillian nodded as they moved up the sidewalk, but she couldn't help thinking how much she hated all this lying. "Couldn't we just tell them the truth?" she asked plaintively. "Surely they would understand."

Zach raked a hand through his hair. "Yeah, you're probably right. We'll see how it goes. Maybe, if the right opening comes, we can tell them." Somehow she didn't feel any better.

As before Zach rang the doorbell, then opened the door and ushered Jillian inside. As before, the entry hall was dark and cool. The television was on in the den, and one of the kids yelled from upstairs. Zach called out his brother's name, Sharon appeared at the end of the hall.

"Oh, hi, y'all. Come on in. Brett's got the barbecue fired up out back. How do ribs sound?"

"Great," Zach said heartily, slapping his middle and ushering Jillian down the hallway.

One moment all was quiet and normal, but then they stepped into the den and chaos erupted.

"Surprise!"

Bodies seemed to hurl at them from all directions. Jillian instinctively latched onto Zach, hearing him exclaim, "Mom! Dad?"

It took several moments for Jillian to realize that the gifts stacked on all the tables in the room and that the congratulations raining down on them from all directions were part of a surprise wedding shower masterminded by her two sisters-in-law and that the middle-aged couple throwing their arms around her and Zach were none other than Zach's parents.

"What are you doing here?" Zach was exclaiming, holding his father at arm's length. Mr. Keller was a weathered, thicker, slightly gray version of his middle son. Mrs. Keller owned her son's vibrant green eyes and wore her thick reddish-brown hair in a swinging cut that reached just below her chin. She was a tallish woman who filled out her jeans and western shirt with slender curves.

"What do you think?" his father replied, grinning. "Had to meet my new daughter, didn't I? Congratulations, son! We're so happy for you!"

His mom smiled almost shyly at Jillian. "Such a pretty face! My stars those eyes take your breath away!"

Horrified, Jillian just stared, stunned to her toes. Then Zach picked a note of normalcy and said affectionately, "Yeah, they have that effect on me, too." He slid an arm around Jillian's waist and bent to kiss his mother's cheek. "Mom, this is Jillian. Honey, these are my parents, Dante and Beth."

Jillian swallowed and found her voice. "So nice to meet you, Mr. and Mrs. Keller." Suddenly she was scooped away from Zach by strong arms folding her into a hug.

"Make it 'Dad and Mom,'" Dante Keller said, a catch thickening his voice.

"Welcome to the family, darling," Beth said, taking her turn to hug her like a long lost daughter.

Jillian suddenly felt tears spilling from her eyes. Zach was there again an instant later, pulling her against him. "I don't know what to say," he told the room at large. "We're just blown away, both of us."

Jillian nodded against his shoulder, sniffed, and lifted her head. "We didn't want any fuss," she said shakily. "You've gone to so much trouble." She looked around, seeing in the kind, happy faces around her the death of any hopes of ending the charade. She didn't know if she was glad or sad.

"Marriages deserve celebration," Beth Keller said animatedly.

"And we know from experience how much stuff you need when you first set up housekeeping," Sharon said. "Zach's just been camping out all this time, and you said yourself you'd been living with your sister until just a few weeks before the wedding, so we figure you need plenty."

"Which means it's gift time!" Mary announced, pushing her pregnant bulk through the crowd to snag Jillian by the hand. Jillian grabbed desperately at Zach as she was towed away. To her relief, Zach ducked under arms and wove through bodies to wrap an arm around her waist. He stayed glued to her side during the next hour as they opened package after package and endured joke after newlywed joke. Zach introduced her to so many people that her head was reeling with names and faces, not to mention the array of gadgets and linens, cookbooks and dishware, greeting cards, decor items—some of them absolutely bizarre—and gag gifts that were heaped on them.

Jillian began to relax about halfway through dinner. It was just impossible not to enjoy the celebratory mood. Despite the melting heat, Sharon and Brett had decorated the backyard with hanging lights and folded paper wedding bells. They'd set up tables and folding chairs, laid out pristine white paper tablecloths and made centerpieces of plastic doves and dried flowers. The paper plates were printed with hearts and wedding rings linked with flowing ribbons. Citronella candle torches kept the winged pests away. Sharon and Mary and Beth had laid out a feast of baked potatoes, salad, baked beans and rack upon rack of barbecued ribs that Dante and Brett grilled over charcoal while Daniel kept everyone's glasses full of iced tea so sweet it made Jillian's teeth ache. After they'd stuffed themselves to the gills, Beth and Sharon brought out a miniature wedding cake from a local bakery and served it up with homemade ice cream.

For a while that evening, laughter, the company of family and friends and the possessive closeness of her husband completely filled Jillian's consciousness. Only later, when the crowd began to thin out and the family gathered around the table with cold drinks in hand, sleepy children draped over their shoulders and laps, did Jillian begin to feel the guilt creep in once more. She was lying to these dear, generous people, pretending to be a permanent part of their family, and it was so wonderful to feel a part of a real family again! But it was a lie, a game, and it was going to break her heart and wound the others. She wanted to weep for all of them.

She wanted it to be real.

Later, driving home with the trunk and back seat of the car packed with gifts, Zach was uncharacteristically quiet. Jillian left him to his thoughts, too overcome by her own to make small talk. Eventually, the silence wore on her nerves so much that she reached for the radio, but Zach surprised her by catching her hand and folding it into his own.

"I'm sorry about tonight," he said softly. "I never dreamed they were planning anything like that."

"There's nothing to be sorry about," she said, "except—"

"Except?"

She couldn't look at him and say it. "You're so lucky to have your parents."

After a moment, he said silkily, "They're crazy about you. It's going to kill them if we end it."

"If?" she said, wheeling her head around, hope springing to life.

His green eyes iced, and his lean mouth firmed. "When," he amended brusquely. "I meant when."

Despondent, she turned away before he could see the sheen of tears in her eyes. "When," she echoed dully. "Yes, of course."

When. When it was over. She wondered, not for the first time, if the price of the safety afforded her by this marriage wasn't too high for both of them—much too high.

Chapter Ten

Zach's parents left for Montana again on Wednesday. He and Jillian took them to the airport, as requested, and a tearful leave-taking was the result. He used Jillian's work and impending opening to put off their invitation to come north for a visit before the end of summer. They had visited the apartment on Tuesday to get a look at what she was doing and were suitably impressed, both by her sculpture and his new home. Jillian had seemed pleased yet oddly depressed at the same time. The tears she wept at their departure lingered on the drive home, and Zach didn't know how to comfort her. He was walking a fine line these days, playing the loving, affectionate husband in public, keeping his distance in private.

To make his misery complete, Eibersen showed up at his office that day, demanding to speak to Jillian and accusing Zach of keeping her prisoner somewhere. Zach took perverse pleasure in tossing the nut out, but Eibersen's parting shot was that he'd get the truth from Camille if it was the last thing he ever did. After Padgett's experience with Eibersen over the weekend, Zach felt obligated to call Camille and warn her. He got a dressing down for his trouble. She accused him of everything from stealing her sister—as if Jillian were an object that could be owned by one individual—to sending Eibersen after her. Despite wanting to throttle her himself, he felt that he had no option but to assign a man to watch over her for her own protection. He decided not to say anything to Jillian about it. She had enough to worry about.

Zach's work had always been a matter of juggling a number of jobs at one time, but Jillian was used to a more peaceful existence. He couldn't help reflecting that these days were more stressful than usual, however. It was all he could do to keep everything in the air, and it was largely thanks to Janzen Eibersen. Funny that he should be beginning to identify with Eibersen in some ways. They were both obsessed with Jillian, and they both loathed Camille. And Jillian didn't want either of them. In case he should ever doubt it, she reminded him repeatedly during those next days.

Jillian worked like a madwoman, coming out of her studio only long enough for meals, showers and sleep. Even at that, Zach ate his meals alone. It was like living with a ghost who cooked and ran water and operated power tools.

Thankfully, Denise and Worly came over one evening to discuss the upcoming opening of the Art Bar, which meant that Jillian had to behave as though she actually knew he existed. Despite the fact that Zach had called down to alert the front desk of their arrival, they made such a disreputable appearance that he had to go down and identify them before they were allowed to come up. They came armed with pizza and beer, as if Zach and Jillian couldn't be trusted to offer them refreshment to their liking, but Zach was so glad to be in the same room with his own wife for a change that he'd have welcomed them if they'd brought live snakes.

Denise wandered around the apartment, alternately approving and turning up her nose, while Worly investigated Zach's sound system and music collection as if contemplating buying it—or stealing it. Finally they all gathered in the living room, where Worly enjoyed sprawling on the sofa with Denise, leaving only the chair for Zach and Jillian. Zach didn't mind in the least, until Jillian picked a spot in the center of the floor and curled up on the carpet. Conversation was lively and mostly conducted in a language foreign to Zach.

"Jammers are steaming, man. Wait'll you taste. This session'll do us all."

"I'm pumping myself. I mean, the paint is dry and hungry. Can't wait!"

"I'm looking forward to it, too," Jillian said mildly. "But what about the view?"

This went on for some time before Zach figured out they were discussing the upcoming opening and a special viewing to be held by the owner of the Art Bar. When he realized they were talking about picking up Jillian and taking her to the viewing themselves, he put his foot down. "No way. If this guy wants to see what he's getting beforehand, and I can certainly understand that, he'll just have to come here."

To his surprise, Jillian was the one to object. "I'll be perfectly safe with Denise and Worly around!"

"I don't think you should even be going to the opening," Zach countered. "Eibersen knows about it. Who's to say he won't know about this viewing? If you insist on going, I'll have to cancel a couple of things and go with you since it's in the daytime."

"Better listen to the man," Worly counseled. "He knows his stuff."

Jillian sighed and capitulated. For the second time, Zach wanted to hug his unlikely ally, witch hair, tattoos, body piercings and all.

To Jillian's surprise, Mr. Considine, the owner of the Art Bar, made no demur about coming to the apartment to view her work. To her absolute shock, he bought the newly completed piece for three-hundred and fifty dollars and took everything else she had to display for sale. She was so jubilant about this unexpected turn of events that she couldn't keep it to herself and broke her own vow to keep out of Zach's way by practically assaulting him with the news the moment he arrived home. Seeming as delighted as she, he swept her into his arms and whirled her around the room. Suddenly the air was charged with their own peculiar brand of electricity. Setting her on her feet, he brushed the tendrils of hair about her face with his fingertips.

"I'm so proud of you," he said. "Beautiful, sweet and talented, what more could a man want?"

Perhaps it was sheerest folly, but she couldn't stop herself from asking hopefully, "Do you want me, Zach?"

His hands dropped to her shoulders and tightened them. "You know I do."

She went up on tiptoe, lifting her mouth toward his—and his cell phone rang. Cursing, he jerked away and whipped the thing off his belt, and barked into it, "What?"

The color leeched out of his face as he listened to whoever was on the other end. After a moment he asked, "Are you sure you're okay?" He listened again and hung up, clearly alarmed.

"What is it?"

He licked his lips and rubbed a hand over his face before answering. "We've lost Eibersen. He's been acting strange ever since he showed up at my office. I've had a guy shadowing his every move. Obviously Eibersen made him. He lured the op into an abandoned warehouse and locked him up. Thankfully he had his cell phone, but by the time he got someone there to turn him loose again, Eibersen had disappeared. His room is empty. His car's been sold. He's gone completely to ground." Zach rubbed a hand over the back of his neck and seemed to make a sudden decision. "We've got to find him." He kissed her absently in the center of her forehead, told her to stay inside and then said that she shouldn't worry about supper for him. He'd get something somewhere if he had time. With that, he left her to wonder what might have happened if Janzen Eibersen had just stayed home and gotten drunk one more night.

Zach came in late the Sunday night before the Monday opening of the Art Bar and collapsed. He'd done everything possible to find Janzen Eibersen, but it was as if the man had fallen off the face of the earth. He'd even called on every possible source to make a dependable connection in Alaska and checked things from that end, but if Eibersen had made that move, his new employer knew nothing about it yet. Zach felt in his bones that Eibersen was planning something, but he couldn't figure what, which was no surprise since he hadn't been able to figure this case from the beginning. It just didn't fit any of the established patterns in his experience, and he didn't know what to do about it. His strongest instinct, at this point, was to forbid Jillian to even participate in the opening, but he didn't have the heart to do that, and he suspected it would be a waste of breath anyway. He sensed that she'd endured about as much "protection" as she could. So, he only had one choice. He had to get enough rest to be in top form on Monday evening. Everything depended on that now.

Unfortunately, Jillian, who was asleep when he finally came home, had no idea what he was planning, so naturally she woke him on Monday morning to tell him he'd overslept. He mumbled something about not going in and needing sleep, but he didn't ask her to call Lois and explain, so Lois called him on the cell phone in a near panic. His empty belly did the rest, and Jillian found him stumbling around in the kitchen a few minutes later. She whipped him up a quick breakfast, without the coffee, and talked him into taking to the bed for the day. As he slipped between the cool sheets, so redolent of her scent, and laid his head on her pillow, a desperate need assailed him, but exhaustion won, and he slipped into a deep sleep punctuated with erotic longings and dreams. He awoke, late in the afternoon, to the familiarity of his own bed for the first time in weeks. After a quick shower and shave, meant as much to rid him of the lingering effects of his dreams as to clean up, he found his wife in the living room watching an afternoon talk show.

She popped up to make him a snack in order to tide him over until the dinner they'd planned with his brothers and their wives to celebrate her opening. Afterward, they sat together on the sofa and watched the early news, surprised to hear Camille mention that night's opening of the Art Bar. Jillian's nervousness translated itself into constant fidgeting with her glasses, which she'd lately taken to wearing again. Finally, Zach suggested that she have a long soak in preparation for the evening, and went so far as to pour her a glass of white wine to sip while enjoying her bath.

Two hours later, Jillian emerged like a butterfly from a cocoon. She had chosen the dress for the occasion while still living with

Denise and Worly; Denise had hoped that a shopping trip would cheer up her friend. Zach could not fault either decision. The slip dress hugged Jillian's slender curves like shiny, cherry-red skin, dipping low both front and back, displaying the tops of her firm breasts and the graceful sweep of her shoulder blades. A flaring tunic of sheer gold print with a wedding ring collar that buttoned at the back and long, flowing sleeves disguised some of the bare skin but none of her breathtaking shape exposed by the dress itself. A pair of the most ridiculous shoes he'd ever seen completed the ensemble. Shiny red vinyl with ankle straps and faux tortoiseshell platforms with clunky three-inch heels should not have looked both funky and sexy, but on Jillian they somehow did. Her hair had grown long enough to wisp around her neck as well as her face, and she had painted a few tiny streaks of gold glitter through the soft caramel tresses. An earthy brown eye shadow, black mascara and cherry-red lipstick constituted her makeup. He noted that her red toenails were painted red.

"Wow," he said. "Your fairy godmother must be proud."

She laughed. "Didn't you know? We modern Cinderellas don't need fairy godmothers. We do, however, need a little assistance with the modern version of the glass slipper. They aren't securely buckled, would you mind?"

"Not in the least." He got down on one knee and carefully buckled the clear vinyl straps, admiring the trim ankles decorated by the outlandish red vinyl roses. He couldn't help noticing that the creamy expanse of her long legs were bare of stockings, and his temperature rose accordingly. "I'm not sure I can do you justice tonight," he told her huskily, rising to his feet.

She smiled and somehow managed a curtsy in that short skirt and those tall shoes. "Oh, we'll find something for you," she said. "Let's take a look in your closet."

He was only too happy to accept her assistance—until she laid out what she'd chosen. Looking doubtfully at the pale chinos and the once white T-shirt now yellowed to a matching hue, he lifted a skeptical eyebrow. When she came out with the baggy camel tan coat that had once belonged to his father and the green-and-gold paisley vest he had received as a gift and never worn, he actually balked. "This stuff is so old it ought to be tossed," he told her.

"But it's good quality," she said. "The people I know would buy it at resale in a heartbeat. Come on, just try it on."

While he did so, she rummaged around and came up with a ten-year-old pair of brown Italian loafers and a hemp belt. He was stunned by what greeted him in the mirror. "Well, all right," he said skeptically, "if it's what you think best." Was that really him? He looked like something in one of the trendier men's magazines. Didn't he?

She seemed pleased, so he squelched his doubts and went along. When they walked into the restaurant to encounter his brothers and sisters-in-laws, his doubts were put to rest.

"Heavenly days," Mary exclaimed, "you both look like fashion models!"

"I think we're hanging with the 'in' crowd," Brett teased.

"How on earth do you walk in those shoes?" Daniel asked Jillian.

"Very gracefully, obviously," Sharon said. Then she gave Zach a thorough going-over and announced, "I think I married the wrong brother."

Everyone laughed, and the server came with additional menus. Almost ninety minutes and a dangerous amount of prime rib later, Sharon glanced at her watch and announced that they just had time to get the baby-sitter home before her curfew. All rose to leave. Brett apologized for not being able to make the opening itself. "Maybe if it had been on a weekend," he said.

"There will be other showings," Zach assured him, convinced that he was right. Jillian had a unique and sizable talent.

Mary patted her big belly and confessed, "I don't think I'd fit in too well with the crowd tonight anyway. Heck, I don't even fit too well in my own skin these days."

Jillian kissed her on the cheek and told her to take it easy in the draining heat. Thanks, congratulations and good wishes were exchanged, along with hugs and pats. It was almost ten by the time they left the parking lot of the fashionable West End steak house. It was almost ten-thirty before Zach gave up trying to find a closer space and parked the convertible in front of Denise and

Worly's apartment building. As they walked the three blocks to the club, Zach caught Jillian's hand in his, and she neither pulled away nor stiffened.

When they reached the club, they had to work their way through a throng of patrons to the doorman, who expected a cover charge. When Jillian told him that she was one of the artists, he sent inside for confirmation, and the owner, Mr. Considine, showed up himself to escort them inside. Zach thought he was the least likely Deep Ellum club owner imaginable. A short, paunchy, balding man wearing an execrable suit of pale-green polyester over a Hawaiian shirt, he talked too loud and smelled of tobacco, but he seemed to know his business. The place was packed.

Part art deco and part fantasy forest, the gallery consisted of balconies constructed of brushed steep pipe around three sides of the cavernous room. The bar occupied the fourth wall, all burnished mahogany and sparkling mirrors. The spacious dance floor was ringed with cement tree trunks that provided display bases for the club's permanent art collection. Green potted trees, some fifteen feet tall, were interspersed throughout the seating section, sheltering tables and chairs with branches strewn with twinkling lights. The stage, or performance space, was a black rectangle at the apex of the dance floor. The entire wall behind it was draped with black velvet curtains that puddled on the black enameled floor. It was here that the band would begin tuning up in another thirty minutes or so.

Meanwhile, Mr. Considine escorted Jillian and Zach through the gallery exhibits. Zach was amazed to see the number of small red Sold stickers adorning much of the artwork. Denise had sold a piece and was thrilled beyond words. Her wild red hair bounced and wavered in the set lights, her exuberance almost making Zach overlook the plain, skintight, black jersey dress that she wore with black high-topped athletic shoes and mismatched socks. She looked like a lump of coal with feet on one side and red seaweed on the other.

Jillian, to his delight and her own, had sold several pieces, more than anyone except a scruffy, nervous middle-aged man with a white ponytail whose specialty was casting and carving glass into fanciful, colorful shapes. He and Jillian were talking shop in front of an audience of several enthralled patrons when Camille showed up with a camera crew. She was overdressed in floor-length navy satin, and the perfection of her hair and makeup gave her the aura and warmth of a mannequin. As Camille positioned herself with her microphone and the filming lights glared, Zach quickly stepped away to use his cell phone. A short, discreet conversation assured him that Camille's frustrated "protection" was lurking just outside the doors of the packed club. Zach promised to alert him when she left and got off the phone before Jillian or Camille could notice.

Camille did her piece on the trendy and experimental new Art Bar opening in Deep Ellum and dispensed the crew to film extraneous shots. A clearly befuddled Jillian introduced her sister to the glass sculptor, only to have Camille freeze him so deeply that he took himself off, muttering about the "establishment invasion." Zach took note of Camille's combative stance and moved in to be on hand if Jillian should need him.

"So how is married life?" was her opening volley, the tone of manufactured boredom failing to override that of resentment.

Jillian lied smoothly. "Surprisingly easy. I know why my husband's such a great guy now. His family has just been wonderful."

Camille did not bother to reply to such disappointing news. Stepping close she hissed, "You might at least have gotten me an invitation to your opening! Everybody at the office just assumed—"

"But, Camille," Jillian said in surprised exasperation, "no invitations were sent out."

"What?" Camille reeled in obvious shock. "B-but the openings of art shows are always by invitation only."

Jillian shook her head, explaining, "The whole concept behind the Art Bar is one of allowing the public easy access to art. Worly was emphatic that it be a public opening, and the interest in the project was so overwhelming that Mr. Considine was convinced. No one needed an invitation."

Camille had the look of someone who'd been bamboozled. Here she thought she'd been cut out of an elitist, invitation-only event, and it turned out that anyone with the price of admission could get in. To make matters worse, she'd finagled her way in with a film crew and unwittingly given the occasion coverage. And, as usual, it was all Jillian's fault. "You could have paid me the courtesy of a telephone call to explain the situation, you know!"

"It never occurred to me that you had the least interest in it," Jillian told her gently. "You've derided the notion from the beginning."

Zach was enjoying himself too much at this point to keep quiet. He stepped to Jillian's side and slid a possessive arm around her waist, taking great pleasure in informing Camille that her sister was a great success. "She's sold the majority of her work already, and Considine himself bought the central piece for his permanent collection."

"How exciting," Camille drawled, but what she was really saying was, "there's just no accounting for taste."

It was then that Worly's band, nameless by design, took the stage. The houselights went down and a strobe came on over the dance floor. Zach was wrong to think they'd do anything as pedestrian as tune up. They simply picked up their instruments and launched into a garbled, guitar-shrieking song. Thankfully the balcony floor and the "forest" protected them somewhat from the worst of it. Camille rolled her eyes. "I knew that creature Worly wasn't capable of making real music."

Once her friend was insulted, Jillian had apparently had enough. "Listen, Camille," she said caustically, "now that you know you weren't slighted in any way you can care about, why don't you just go and let us enjoy our evening."

To everyone's surprise, apparently even her own, Camille teared up. "How would you know what I care about?" she asked, lifting her chin regally, as if by that action alone she could keep the tears from falling. "All my life I've tried to be somebody others would admire and love, while you get those things without even lifting a finger. It all comes so easily to you. Everybody loves Jillian."

"Except you!" Jillian shot back.

Camille stamped a foot, exclaiming, "Especially me!" The

effect of the music was such that no one even turned a head. "Don't you think I've wanted to hate you? You were Daddy's little darling, but he could barely stand the sight of me."

"That isn't true," Jillian argued. "He just had a hard time being as much a part of your life as he wanted because of your mother."

"When he left, Mother was all I had!" Camille pointed out. "It wasn't my fault they couldn't be in the same room together!"

She was right, of course, though Zach hated to admit it.

Jillian sighed and caught her sister by the upper arm, shaking her gently. "Camille, Daddy and Mom both taught me to love and admire you. I've thanked God for you a million times, and I'll always love you because you are my sister, but it's time you dealt with some important issues from the past. I don't think we can be as close as we both want to be until you do."

Camille regarded her with tears trembling prettily on her lashes, bottom lip quivering. "You mean it? You haven't just written me off?"

Jillian looked her in the eye, saying flatly, "Never. You're my sister."

Camille's vaunted ego summarily reasserted itself. She tossed her golden head. "I'll think about it," she said. "Maybe you're right."

Jillian's lips quirked in a quickly disciplined smile. "That's all I ask." In her wisdom, she had made herself sound the penitent, when they all knew that was not the case, even if Camille couldn't admit it.

They all stood a moment longer, clutching the railing around the balcony as the dance floor filled with gyrating bodies, before Camille pulled in a deep breath and haughtily took her leave, declaring that she couldn't stand one more minute of that "obscene noise." She signaled her crew and was gone without so much as a farewell. Zach reached for his cell phone. Just then a young man wearing a black suit at least two sizes too large for him appeared at Jillian's elbow.

"Mr. Considine asked me to tell you that he reserved a table for you."

Nodding, she allowed him to lead them down the stairs and

into the live forest. Bringing up the rear, Zach quickly made his call and alerted his man that Camille was on her way out.

The table to which they were escorted boasted a placard reading Ms. Jillian Keller, Artist, and Zachary Keller, Husband. Jillian apologized, feeling that it somehow belittled Zach, but he just laughed. "What makes you think that I mind being known as your husband?" He had to shout the question, but the look she gave him in reply was both eloquent and steamy. A thrill shot through him. The hope he had so carefully tried not to nurture these past days flared into stubborn life. They sat in the dark beneath the trees, pretending to enjoy the deafening music and sip complimentary drinks in which neither was particularly interested, until Zach simply couldn't stand it anymore.

"I want to dance with you," he said, getting up. She looked up, clearly surprised, but placed her hand in his.

He led her out onto the periphery of the dance floor. All around them couples were gyrating as if in the various throes of convulsions, but he didn't care. Not even the screaming, screeching music could convince him that he shouldn't take her into his arms and dance with her just the way he wanted. As her willingness to have him do so became obvious, the music actually seemed to recede, taking everything and everyone else with it. All alone in a world of their own making, they wrapped each other close and danced to the tune of their hearts. After the demise of the frantic piece, Worly, bless his aberrant soul, moved the band into a slow number, surprising Zach with his deep, gravelly vocals. The song itself was ridiculous, the lyrics unfathomable—something about goldfish, as far as Zach could tell—but it gave Zach a very good reason to keep his wife in his arms, and when the moment came, only minutes into it, to kiss her, he didn't hesitate.

If anyone paid them the slightest attention, they never noticed, so wrapped up in each other were they. When at last the music ended, Zach bucked up his courage and suggested they go home. Jillian dazzled him with her smile.

"Just let me visit the ladies' room first."

He kissed her again before he could let her go, and he knew then that it was going to be all right. Somehow, he'd married the one woman in the world who could truly make him happy, and she seemed to be giving him the chance to repay her in kind.

Jillian slipped toward the ladies' room on a cloud of euphoria. He did want her. She knew it. Love emanated from him like perfume from a rose. She was so thrilled that she didn't notice the man stepping out of the shadows until she'd bumped into him.

"Sorry."

"You don't have to apologize to me, Jillian."

His hand fastened around her wrist, and she found herself staring into the face of Janzen Eibersen. He'd cut his hair close to the scalp, disguising its paleness and accentuating his dark brows. She realized suddenly that she'd glimpsed him several times that evening and not once recognized him or sensed his proximity.

"What are you doing? Let go of me!" she insisted as he pulled her toward the door.

"Don't fight me if you want to see your sister again," he warned.

Camille. Jillian's blood ran cold. "What have you done with her?"

"Never fear. I only want to talk to you, make you see that you can't let her keep calling the shots." He pulled her into the darkened foyer and past the doorman.

"What are you talking about? Camille has no control over me."

"Oh, please. You forget that I was there, darling Jill. I saw the way she manipulates and bullies you." He pushed her through the door and out onto the sidewalk.

"Not any longer. I put an end to that when I moved out of the house."

"Then why did you let her bully you into marrying her hand-picked bodyguard?"

"You've got it all wrong," Jillian said desperately, afraid to fight and afraid to let him haul her down the sidewalk away from Zach. "Camille didn't want us to marry. She refused to even come to the wedding."

He stopped long enough to look down at her. "What? Then you did it on your own? You married him on your own?"

"Of course I did!"

"By why? *Why?*"

She could have told him that she'd had no choice, but she knew now that wasn't true, no matter what she'd told herself at the time. "Because I love him," she said simply.

Janzen seemed terribly shaken. "You can't!" he exclaimed, clearly puzzled. "You love me! I know you do."

Jillian shook her head. "No."

"But you were so kind. Camille would cut me to the quick, and you were always there to make it better, always on my side."

"I felt sorry for you," she said gently.

"B-but—"

"Jan, think! I know much of it must be lost in an alcoholic haze, but how could you forget all those times you tried to...to get close to me? Did I ever let you kiss me, even once? Did I even let you touch me? No. I told you over and over again that I didn't want that!"

"But that's you, Jillian! Your innate decency, your—"

"For Pete's sake, Janzen, will you wake up! I never let you or anybody else touch me, but I've been throwing myself at Zach from the moment I met him!"

"And from now on I promise to do a better job of catching you," Zach said, stepping out of the shadows between two buildings. Gabler was with him and a man Jillian didn't recognize.

"Zach!" Jillian cried, reaching out for him.

Janzen pulled her back. Zach ambled closer. "You've got your hands on my wife, Eibersen. I don't much like the idea." Suddenly Zach's fist flashed and Jan was looking up from the ground, his hand cradling his chin. Jillian didn't bother to inspect the damage. She leaped over him and into her husband's arms.

"Zach, he has Camille! He must've got her when she left earlier! He—"

"No, he doesn't," Zach assured her, folding her close. "Camille is at home getting ready for bed. I just talked to the guy I've had on her these past few days."

Relief and rage warred inside Jillian. Rage won. She turned on Janzen. "How dare you frighten me like that?"

"I never said I had her," Janzen whined. "I just said you should come with me if you wanted to see her again."

Jillian drew back her foot and kicked him.

"Ow!" He sat up, grabbing his knee. "Those shoes are dangerous!"

"Not nearly so dangerous as me," Zach drawled, draping a calming arm over Jillian's shoulders. "I believe I promised to break both your arms if you ever touched Jillian again."

"Zach, no," Jillian whispered. "He isn't worth the trouble it would cause."

"I believe you're right, sweetheart," he told her. "So, Eibersen, I'll make you another promise, instead. So much as contact her, and I'll see you behind bars if I have to build my own jail. You got that?"

Janzen nodded and stuffed his hand into his jacket pocket. Jillian stiffened, and Gabler pounced, easily wrestling Janzen to the ground again. He came up with two envelopes.

"They're just airline tickets!" Janzen muttered into the cement. Gabler handed them over to Zach, who flipped them open, saw that they were airline tickets and nodded to Gabe to let Jan go.

Janzen rolled over and sat up with a huff, demanding petulantly, "What am I supposed to do with them now? I thought the two of us would start a new life in Alaska together. I spent everything I had on those!"

Zach handed them back to Gabler, who got up, apparently satisfied that Jan was unarmed. "You're going to use one of them," Zach said. "I'll buy the other one from you for Padgett here."

Jan looked at the other man. "You! I remember you!"

Padgett nodded sheepishly and reached down to help Jan up. "Yeah, yeah, we're old friends. Consider me your personal bodyguard."

"Padgett will see you safely to Alaska," Zach announced. "Don't think you can slip back without my knowing it. I've got a man looking out for you there now."

Jan brushed himself off glumly. "I could've had her if you hadn't come in and turned her head," he muttered.

"Not on your best day," Jillian told him curtly.

"The point is," Zach said, "she's mine now." He looked at Jillian and added, "And I'll never let her go without a fight."

She caught her breath, tears starting in her eyes. "Zachary Keller, I love you!"

"I love you, too, baby, more every day."

"Let's go home."

Zach got out of the car, handed the keys to the valet and hurried around to sweep his bride into his arms. She laughed as her feet left the ground. "How did you know I was with Jan?" she asked. He sensed that it was a way to hold the excitement at bay just a little longer.

"Are you kidding? I haven't taken my eyes off you all evening. If I had, I might have noticed him earlier. As it was, I realized the instant you bumped into him that I'd let him get too close. I'm sorry for that, sweetheart. It won't happen again."

She laid her head on his shoulder as he carried her through the lobby. "When is he leaving for Alaska?"

"The tickets were for 2:00 a.m. By then, we'll *really* be husband and wife."

She lifted her head, frowning. "What do you mean by that?"

He grinned and kissed her. "You know exactly what I mean. Hello, Eugene."

"Mr. Keller, Mrs. Keller." The security guard hurried to punch up the elevator for them, rocking on his toes and grinning unabashedly while they waited. "How was your evening?"

"A great success," Zach answered as the elevator doors slid open and he carried her aboard. "My wife's a famous artist, you know."

"Oh, I'm not," she protested. "It was my very first—" He kissed her to halt the flow of self-deprecating words, and he kept kissing her until the elevator stopped and they had to get off.

He let her down while he unlocked the door, pleased to see that her knees were so weak she had to lean against the wall for support.

"You're acting very strange," she said suspiciously.

"Am I?" he answered. "Well, you'd better get used to it. This, I'm afraid, is what a happy Zach acts like." She was still laughing when he swept her up once more and carried her across the threshold. "Welcome home, sweetheart." In reply, she wrapped her arms around his neck and kissed him lingeringly on the mouth. He made straight for the bedroom, determined that he'd slept his last night on that damned couch.

There, by the light spilling through the door from the tiny setback hall, he began systematically undressing her, shoes first. He didn't have much to do. She was wearing just three pieces of clothing, the sheer tunic, the dress and a pair of familiar-looking pink panties. He laid her back on the bed and began peeling off his own clothes, telling her how beautiful she was and how much he loved her. She lay open to his inspection, her mouth curled in a soft smile, the twin fires of love and desire burning in her big blue eyes. When he was naked, he spread her legs with his hands and came down between them. Perhaps he should slow down, he worried, prepare her better. But then she wrapped her arms around and drew up her legs, positioning herself perfectly.

His chest was so tight he could barely breathe, his heart pounding like the trap set in Worly's band. He was afraid he would cry. Swallowing down a doughy lump in his throat, he whispered, "Jillian, will you marry me, *really* marry me, now, here, forever?"

Her smile was utterly serene. "Oh, yes."

He could see it in her eyes. Eibersen and the threat he had represented was gone. The only reason they had for staying together now was love, mutual and strong. He pushed into her as slowly as he could bear. She winced when he broke through, then put back her head and laughed throatily. He laid his face against her neck and sighed with the deepest satisfaction he'd ever known, and then he began, ever so gently, ever so thoroughly, to make mad, passionate love to his wife. Somewhere in the midst of it came the thought that they just might take that trip to Montana this summer after all.

And maybe next summer three of them would be making the trip. But that was a decision he had no right to make on his own.

He made himself slow down and pull back, smoothing a wisp of hair from her cheek. "You said before that we shouldn't take a chance on making a baby."

Jillian's smile was slow and rich with a uniquely earthy wisdom. "That was before," she said, "before I found enough courage to tell you how much I love you."

"Before you made me the world's happiest man, you mean."

To his delight, she laughed that deep, throaty laugh of hers and wrapped herself around him even more tightly. "If we had a baby, we'd have to move again."

"Oh, no, not that!" he teased.

"I suppose my sister would always take us in."

"Oh, no, not that!" he said in genuine horror this time.

She laughed again, and it was so wonderful to hear, so right. Then he set himself once more to pleasing the woman who had finally made his life complete, and the next sound that rolled up out her throat was the sweetest kind of sensual music for a man and woman in love.

*   *   *   *   *

Be sure to look for a new book by Arlene James, coming in December from Silhouette Special Edition.

Silhouette ROMANCE™

SOMETIMES THE SMALLEST PACKAGES CAN LEAD TO THE BIGGEST SURPRISES!

Join *Silhouette Romance* as more couples experience the joy only babies can bring!

Bundles of JOY

July 1999
BABIES, RATTLES AND CRIBS... OH MY!
by Leanna Wilson (SR #1378)

His baby girl had suddenly appeared on his doorstep, and Luke Crandall needed daddy lessons—fast! So lovely Sydney Reede agreed to help the befuddled bachelor. But when baby cuddles turned into grown-up kisses, Sydney wondered if what Luke really wanted was *her!*

August 1999
THE BILLIONAIRE AND THE BASSINET
by Suzanne McMinn (SR #1384)

When billionaire Garrett Blakemore set out to find the truth about a possible heir to his family's fortune, he didn't expect to meet a pretty single mom and her adorable baby! But the more time he spent with Lanie Blakemore and her bundle of joy, the more he found himself wanting the role of dad....

And look for more **Bundles of Joy** titles in late 1999:

THE BABY BOND by Lilian Darcy (SR #1390)
in September 1999

BABY, YOU'RE MINE by Lindsay Longford (SR #1396)
in October 1999

Available at your favorite retail outlet.

Silhouette®

If you enjoyed what you just read,
then we've got an offer you can't resist!

Take 2 bestselling
love stories FREE!
Plus get a FREE surprise gift!

Clip this page and mail it to Silhouette Reader Service™

IN U.S.A.
3010 Walden Ave.
P.O. Box 1867
Buffalo, N.Y. 14240-1867

IN CANADA
P.O. Box 609
Fort Erie, Ontario
L2A 5X3

YES! Please send me 2 free Silhouette Romance® novels and my free surprise gift. Then send me 6 brand-new novels every month, which I will receive months before they're available in stores. In the U.S.A., bill me at the bargain price of $2.90 plus 25¢ delivery per book and applicable sales tax, if any*. In Canada, bill me at the bargain price of $3.25 plus 25¢ delivery per book and applicable taxes**. That's the complete price and a savings of over 10% off the cover prices—what a great deal! I understand that accepting the 2 free books and gift places me under no obligation ever to buy any books. I can always return a shipment and cancel at any time. Even if I never buy another book from Silhouette, the 2 free books and gift are mine to keep forever. So why not take us up on our invitation. You'll be glad you did!

215 SEN CNE7
315 SEN CNE9

Name	(PLEASE PRINT)	
Address	Apt.#	
City	State/Prov.	Zip/Postal Code

* Terms and prices subject to change without notice. Sales tax applicable in N.Y.
** Canadian residents will be charged applicable provincial taxes and GST.
   All orders subject to approval. Offer limited to one per household.
   ® are registered trademarks of Harlequin Enterprises Limited.

SROM99   ©1998 Harlequin Enterprises Limited

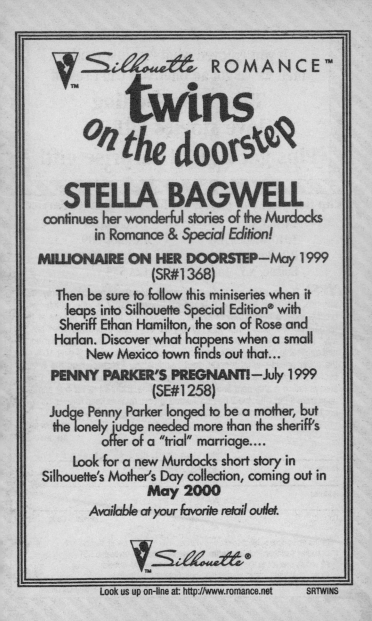

Silhouette ROMANCE™
twins on the doorstep

STELLA BAGWELL

continues her wonderful stories of the Murdocks
in Romance & *Special Edition!*

MILLIONAIRE ON HER DOORSTEP—May 1999
(SR#1368)

Then be sure to follow this miniseries when it
leaps into Silhouette Special Edition® with
Sheriff Ethan Hamilton, the son of Rose and
Harlan. Discover what happens when a small
New Mexico town finds out that...

PENNY PARKER'S PREGNANT!—July 1999
(SE#1258)

Judge Penny Parker longed to be a mother, but
the lonely judge needed more than the sheriff's
offer of a "trial" marriage....

Look for a new Murdocks short story in
Silhouette's Mother's Day collection, coming out in
May 2000

Available at your favorite retail outlet.

Silhouette®

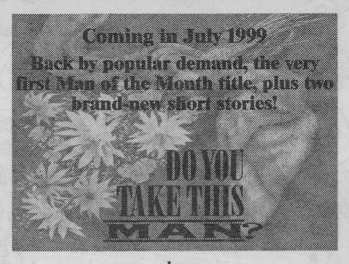